Withdrawn from Stock

D0708191

HITS &
MISSES

Also by Simon Rich

Elliot Allagash
The Last Girlfriend on Earth
What in God's Name
Spoiled Brats
The World of Simon Rich

HITS & MISSES

stories

SIMON RICH

First published in Great Britain in 2018 by Serpent's Tail,
an imprint of Profile Books Ltd
3 Holford Yard
Bevin Way
London
WC1X 9HD
www.serpentstail.com

Copyright © 2018 Simon Rich

'The Foosball Championship of the Whole Entire Universe' and 'The Book
of Simon' previously appeared in *The New Yorker*.

Illustrations by Ed Steed

10 9 8 7 6 5 4 3 2 1

Printed and bound in Great Britain by Clays Ltd, Elcograf S.p.A.

The moral right of the author has been asserted.

The characters and events in this book are fictitious. Any similarity to real
persons, living or dead, is coincidental and not intended by the author.

All rights reserved. Without limiting the rights under copyright reserved
above, no part of this publication may be reproduced, stored or introduced
into a retrieval system, or transmitted, in any form or by any means
(electronic, mechanical, photocopying, recording or otherwise), without the
prior written permission of both the copyright owner and the publisher of
this book.

A CIP record for this book can be obtained from the British Library

ISBN 978 1 78125 905 4
eISBN 978 1 78283 386 4

For my wife and daughter

CONTENTS

THE BABY

It was understood that, when the baby came, Ben's office would become the nursery.

Ben would miss his beloved writing room, but he knew he was making a relatively minor sacrifice. His wife, Sue, had spent the last two years taking stomach-bloating vitamins and getting poked in the vagina by an elderly Polish gynecologist. She'd quit Claritin-D and martinis. The least Ben could do was find some other place to write his novel.

Besides, by the time Sue gave birth, his book would almost certainly be finished. He was already up to the last chapter, and according to Pregnancy.com, the baby was still just the size of a small turnip. He had all the time he needed.

As he leaned back in his custom writing chair, Ben found himself daydreaming about his book's reception. His novels so far had been modestly received, but maybe this one would take him to the proverbial "next level." He pictured himself traveling the world, with Sue and the turnip in tow, on a glamorous international book tour. It was while he was reveling in this fantasy that he caught sight of his watch and remembered that he had somewhere to be.

• • •

"Sorry I'm late!" Ben said as he hustled into the little white room. "I was stuck on the subway for an hour."

"Oh man, that sucks!" Sue said. She kissed Ben on the forehead and he smiled, relieved that she'd accepted his excuse.

"You are just in time," said Dr. Kowalski as he squirted some goo onto Sue's belly.

Sue turned to Ben and giggled. "You ready?"

"Ready," Ben said. He squeezed her hand as a black-and-white image took shape on a nearby monitor. It took some getting used to, but before long, Ben was able to identify the baby's legs and torso.

"What's that thing?" he asked, pointing excitedly to a small white smudge.

"Is penis!" said the doctor triumphantly. "It means you have boy!"

"Whoa!" Ben said as he and Sue laughed with amazement. "A boy!"

Ben pointed at another blurry shape. "What about that thing?"

"Is pencil," said the doctor.

Ben's smile faded. "Did you say *pencil*?"

"Or pen," the doctor said. "Is too early to know at this stage."

"What does it mean?" Ben asked nervously.

Dr. Kowalski grinned.

"It means you have writer!"

That afternoon, Ben spent some more time on Pregnancy.com. He was surprised to learn that a fetus's profession was usually apparent by the sixteenth week of gestation. For example, if you could detect a hoodie in the sonogram, that generally indicated your child was a coder. If your fetus held a tiny plunger, he or she was most likely a plumber, and a gavel almost certainly meant judge. Statistically, writers were less common, although the odds went up significantly if one of the parents was an Ashkenazi Jew.

Ben reached into his pocket and took out the strip of black-and-white photographs Dr. Kowalski had given them. The images were pretty hazy (they'd agreed not to blow $1,400 on the exorbitant, non-insurance-covered "4-D" option). But Ben could still make out a few details, including an open moleskin notebook. He couldn't read the baby's handwriting. Still, he could sense the work was confident. There were very few scratch-outs, and a couple of sentences were underlined. Unlike his father, the fetus didn't seem to have any difficulties focusing.

Ben tossed the pictures into a drawer and slammed it shut, annoyed with himself for wasting the whole day. He turned on his laptop, opened his novel, and stared at the screen, watching the little cursor blink and blink. And blink.

The next day, Sue's mother, Joan, drove in from Scarsdale. She was wearing a sweat suit and flanked by a pair of cowering teenage movers.

"Start clearing out everything!" she shouted as she flung open the door to Ben's office.

"Do we have to do this right now?" Ben asked her gently.

"Why wait?" she said. "The baby's gonna be here before you know it."

She snapped her fingers and the movers jumped swiftly into action, packing Ben's files into cardboard boxes. Ben could feel himself begin to panic. His book was a historical novel—a postcolonial epic about General Custer's last stand. He couldn't finish it without his notes.

"Please," he begged his mother-in-law. "I'm still using everything you're taking."

"You're going to have to get used to this," Joan said in a singsongy voice. "There's going to be a *lot* of changes around here."

"I'm aware," Ben said.

"Instead of that desk, there's gonna be a crib, instead of that printer, there's gonna be diapers, and instead of your novels, there's gonna be *his* novels..."

"Whoa, whoa, whoa," Ben said, waving his arms in the air. "We don't know for sure that the baby is a novelist. He could be any kind of writer. According to Pregnancy.com, there's a forty percent chance he ends up blogging."

Joan rolled her eyes, smiling. "You wish."

"What's that supposed to mean?"

She jabbed him playfully in the ribs. "You're jealous of the baby."

Ben forced a laugh. "That's ridiculous."

"Relax," she said. "It's normal for new fathers to be jealous. Don't worry. When the baby's born, you'll take one look at him and know just what to do—"

"I'm not jealous!" Ben shouted. He flushed with embarrassment. He hadn't meant his denial to come out so aggressively. He shot the teenagers a mitigating smile, but they both avoided eye contact.

"Look, I'm sorry," he said. "I'm right in the middle of a chapter. Can we please just not do this right this second?"

The movers turned to Joan for approval. She groaned histrionically and threw her hands up in the air. "Okay, okay, fine," she said. "But we'll be back."

Ben waited until they were all gone, then yanked open his desk drawer and held the sonogram up to the light. There was only one thought on his mind: *What the hell was that kid writing?*

"I thought you said it was, like, fourteen hundred dollars?" Sue asked as Ben rubbed her stomach with some almond oil.

"It's actually less," he said brightly. "Like, thirteen eighty."

"I don't know," she said. "It seems kind of pricy for a slightly more detailed sonogram picture. I mean, that's like the equivalent of five thousand diapers."

"Damn it!" Ben snapped.

"Whoa!" Sue said, taken aback. "Honey, what's wrong?"

Ben thought for a second.

"I guess I'm just paranoid," he bluffed. "I want to see

7

him—really *see* him—just so I know he's one hundred per-cent all right in there. You know? Just for my own peace of mind."

"Oh, baby!" she said. "I had no idea you were feeling this way." She kissed him loudly on the cheek. "If that's how you feel, then of course. I support you."

Dr. Kowalski was his usual upbeat self as he booted up the high-tech 4-D scanner. But when he put on his glasses and squinted at the screen, his face went slack.

"My God," he murmured softly. "My God in heaven."

"What's wrong?" Sue asked the doctor.

Dr. Kowalski swiveled around and laughed. "I am sorry!" he said. "Everything is fine with baby health! It is just this thing fetus is writing. It is so *engrossing*." He shook his head with amazement. "I forgot there were other people in room! Until you spoke, I was just, like, 'in it'!"

Sue exhaled with relief. She tried to squeeze Ben's hand, but his fingers were limp. He leapt up and hurried toward the scanner. "How did he get that *typewriter*?" he asked.

Dr. Kowalski shrugged. "Is normal at twenty-five weeks."

Ben was disturbed to notice that the fetus was using a hip, vintage Underwood. He was almost certainly a novelist and probably a literary one.

"What's he writing?" he asked, trying to sound casual.

"Is historical novel," said Dr. Kowalski. "About General Custer."

Ben's heart raced. "He's writing about *General Custer*?"

"Yes," said the doctor. "But it is about so much more than that. It is suspenseful, lyrical. In some ways, it is story of America itself."

"Wow!" Sue said. "That sounds pretty good. Right, honey? Right?"

"He stole my idea," Ben murmured as they climbed up to their fifth-floor Brooklyn walk-up.

"How is that even possible?" Sue asked. She was exhausted and a little out of breath.

"They can hear stuff through the womb," Ben said. "He must have heard me talking about it or something."

"But you never talk about your work," Sue reasoned. "I mean, until today, I had no idea you were starting a book about General Custer."

"I'm not starting it; I'm finishing it! I'm up to the last chapter, God damn it!"

"It's going to be fine," she said soothingly. "There can be two books about the same thing, right?"

But Ben had already bounded up the stairs, leaving her to walk up the final flight alone.

Ben raced into his office and did some mental calculations. Even if the fetus was nearing the end of his novel, he was still stuck inside Sue's womb. He wouldn't be able to physically turn in a manuscript until after he was born. Assuming the due date held, Ben had fifteen weeks to finish his draft and submit it first to publishers.

He closed the door and flipped open his laptop. He was about to get to work when his phone began to buzz—an unknown Manhattan number.

"Dr. Kowalski?" he answered wearily.

"I'm sorry, no!" said a polite female voice. "I'm from the Wylie Agency. Is this Ben Herstein?"

Ben stood up with excitement. He was between literary agents and had been hoping for some time for a call like this one.

"Yes, it's me!" he said. "What's up?"

"I'm calling about your son," she said. "I tried to reach him directly, but my understanding is he hasn't yet been born. Anyway, I was wondering if he might be interested in representation."

A knot of tension formed in the center of Ben's spine as the agent praised the fetus's work in progress. Apparently, an unscrupulous nurse had posted the 4-D scan to Reddit, and the link had gone viral.

"He's not interested," Ben said.

"Are you sure?"

"Yes!"

There was a light knock on the door.

"Honey?" Sue asked. "Are you okay?"

"Just leave me alone!" Ben said. "I'm trying to work!"

"Mom and the movers are here," she said. "Remember? To put in the crib?"

Ben whipped open the door. "I've made a decision," he said through gritted teeth. "I'm not giving up my office."

Sue tilted her head, genuinely confused. "I don't understand," she said. "We already talked about this."

She reached for his arm, but he jerked it away.

"Everyone just leave me alone!" he whined.

"Baby, come on—"

He slammed the door, giving himself over to the
tantrum. "No!" he screamed. "No, no, no, no, no!"

Ben spent the third trimester writing incessantly, barely
stopping to sleep and eat. But no matter how frantically he
worked, the fetus kept gaining on him.

In the thirty-sixth week of Sue's pregnancy, *The New Yorker*
published an excerpt from the fetus's unfinished book. Ben
couldn't bring himself to read the entire thing, but he forced
himself to skim the first three columns. It was unbelievably
intimidating. The fetus had boldly chosen to portray General
Custer as gay. Not just a little gay—fully gay. He'd also included a black character, and written his dialogue in dialect,
but somehow managed to pull the thing off tastefully. Ben
flipped to the Contributor's Notes and was horrified to see
that "Unnamed Fetus" was listed as a "Staff Writer." He
cursed out loud and chucked the magazine into the garbage.

As the weeks wore on, Ben found himself spending more
and more time in his office, and less and less time with Sue.
He still massaged her belly every evening, but he rushed
through the ritual like a squeegee man at a red light, calling
it quits after a couple of perfunctory swipes.

At night, while she snored in her Snoogle, he pounded

out page after page, racing toward his novel's denouement. He was nearing the final scene when he heard a soft knock on his door.

"Sweetie?" Sue said. "Can you please come out of there?"

"I'm busy," he said harshly. "Can it wait?"

She let out a sharp breath. "No."

"Look who decided to show up," Joan said, glaring at Ben with undisguised contempt.

Ben avoided eye contact and followed his wife into the delivery room. She was lying on a gurney, surrounded by nurses, anesthesiologists, and Scott Rudin, who was trying to option the fetus's book for a film.

Ben gave his wife's shoulder an obligatory squeeze. "You're doing great," he said. "Great job."

"Where have you been?" she asked.

Ben forced a laugh. "What?" he leaned down and smiled at her. "What do you mean?"

She gripped his hand. Her eyes were soft and glossy from the drugs, and her forehead was beaded with sweat. "I've missed you," she said, her voice breaking. "Where did you go?"

Ben felt his throat go dry. He started to apologize, but before he could get out the words, Sue's body was racked by a violent contraction. He winced as his wife grunted through it, breathing bravely through the spasm of white-hot pain.

"Here it comes!" said Dr. Kowalski. "It's a big one!"

The nurses guided the manuscript out of Sue's vagina,

making sure the title page was facing up. The book was called *Last Stand* and somehow featured an advance blurb from George Saunders.

The baby himself popped out a second later, looking smart but understated in a slim tweed blazer and a pair of Warby Parker glasses. The doctor laid him on his mother's chest. He seemed calm at first, but within moments he began to scream. Sue tried to calm the newborn with a kiss, but the infant kept howling, a wail that built steadily in pitch, like a fast-approaching siren.

"Is this normal?" Ben asked. "What's happening?"

"I do not know," said Dr. Kowalski. His face was pale, and his eyes betrayed a small degree of fear. "It is louder cry than normal. I am not sure what it is."

Ben watched as the baby flailed desperately, grasping at the air with his tiny bluish fingers. He had never seen anyone look so helpless. When the infant turned toward him, his eyes wide with fear, Ben felt an odd sensation in his chest. In a flash, he knew just what to do.

Ben followed his son's gaze across the room, to where the nurse had set aside the manuscript.

"Does anyone have a pen?" he asked.

Joan shook her fist at him. "What do you need a pen for?!"

"Just give me a pen," he said firmly.

Joan raised her eyebrows, taken aback by Ben's confidence. She dug into her purse and handed him a purple Bic.

"He wants to make a revision," Ben explained to the hospital staff. "That's why he's screaming so loud. He's worried the manuscript will go out to critics before he's made the edit."

He carefully placed the pen in his son's hand. The baby gestured frantically at his novel, tears streaming from his frightened eyes.

"I know," Ben said soothingly. "I know. It's hard." He carefully flipped through the pages, making sure the baby had a chance to scan each one. They were six chapters in when the baby started bawling.

"Is it this page?" Ben asked gently. "Is it something on this page?"

The baby sniffled.

"Okay," Ben said. "Shhh. Okay."

He lowered his son to the manuscript and watched as the infant dragged his pen across the page, trimming the final sentence of a dense, descriptive passage.

"Good cut," Ben said, impressed.

The baby let out a long, contented sigh, then fell asleep in his father's arms. Ben studied his son's tiny features. His fuzzy, bulbous cheeks, his softly swelling chest. It was hard to believe this was something he'd helped to create. He turned to his wife and noticed there were tears in her eyes.

"I love you, baby," she said.

"I love you too," he said. "Now come on. Let's get this little guy into his nursery."

THE FOOSBALL CHAMPIONSHIP OF
THE WHOLE ENTIRE UNIVERSE

August 21, 1991
Boca Raton, Florida—Grandma's Rec Room

Tensions will be running high today as the Blue Team, coached by eleven-year-old Nathaniel Rich, takes on the Red Team, coached by seven-year-old Simon Rich.

So far this summer, Nathaniel's Blue Team has dominated Simon's Red Team, winning all eighty-three matches. But the coaches have agreed that since today's showdown is the last game of vacation, it "counts for everything." The brother who wins today's contest will be declared the Foosball Champion of the Whole Entire Universe.

KEYS TO THE GAME

Coaching

Coach Simon is renowned for his fiery devotion to the game of foosball. But while some see his passion as an asset, others view it as a liability.

"Coach cries a lot," observed Red Team halfback Donald Mursgard. "Like, pretty much every time we lose."

Coach Simon's postgame meltdowns have become so violent that League Commissioner Mom has threatened to ban foosball forever. The young coach has promised to "be good," but as his losing streak continues, his outbursts have only intensified.

"The last time we lost," Mursgard recalled, "Coach attacked us. It was scary, because even though he's just a boy, to us, he's a giant—about fifty to sixty times our size. He kept banging his fists against our tiny heads and screaming that we were 'stupid, stupid, stupid.' It wasn't exactly great for team morale."

Right wing Johnny Hult recalled another recent loss. "We were about to win, for the first time all season. But at the last second, the Blue Team's goalie kicked the ball across the entire length of the field, to win the game 10–9. I figured Coach Simon would start screaming, like how he usually does, but instead he got this far-off look in his eyes, like he had seen a ghost. He walked away from the table, and as he was walking he just sort of collapsed. Like, his legs kind of just went out from under him. Then he let out this kind of animal shriek and started tearing at his hair, like literally ripping out entire tufts. It's sort of like he went crazy. Meanwhile, Coach Nathaniel [of the Blue Team] was laughing. It was not a good day for the sport."

Health of Red Team

Coach Simon's decision to physically discipline his players has resulted in several injuries. Center Bert Ragumson is missing both of his legs, halfback Lance Ricardo is playing without a head, and the entire defensive line is fully paralyzed.

Coach Nathaniel's players, meanwhile, remain healthy despite a controversial incident earlier this week when Coach Simon savagely attacked them in order to, in his words, "make it fair."

"It was the scariest moment of my life," said Blue Team goalie Mark McMalley. "Coach Simon picked up a remote control, which for us is like the equivalent of a pretty large tree, and he tried to kill me with it. He tried to bash in my skull. Listen. I'm an athlete, not a psychologist. But it doesn't take a Sigmund Freud to see that this kid needs medication."

Differing Strategies

Stylistically, the Red Team and the Blue Team are a study in contrasts. While Coach Nathaniel favors a finesse game, Coach Simon prefers a more physical style of play.

"He just spins us," explained halfback Carlos Davila. "As hard as he can. Over and over and over. The idea is, I guess, that if we keep doing backflips, sooner or later, one of us will randomly hit the ball forward, with our feet or the back of our head. I don't know how many good men have to get paralyzed before Coach admits that this tactic doesn't work."

Accusations of Misconduct

Coach Simon has repeatedly accused Coach Nathaniel of cheating.

"He cheats all the time," he told reporters, between sobs. "That's how he wins."

When asked to explain specifically how the Blue Team was cheating, Coach Simon declined to elaborate. "He just cheats," Simon said with conviction. "He's a cheater."

Coach Nathaniel has not responded to these allegations.

X Factor

Earlier this week, after another emotional loss to the Blue Team, Coach Simon made the controversial choice to eat the ball.

"It was crazy," recalled Blue Team forward Arnold Munder. "He just shoved it in his mouth and swallowed it."

It is unclear what type of ball will be used for today's game, with both marbles and grapes being discussed as possibilities.

In any case, sources believe that Coach Simon is near his "emotional breaking point" and that another loss could make him "finally completely snap."

Suspicions of Tampering

Earlier this morning, Coach Nathaniel was called in for a secret closed-door meeting with League Commissioner Mom as well as Grandma, the owner of Foosball Stadium.

While it isn't fully known what was discussed, it's rumored that Coach Nathaniel was pressured by league brass to allow Coach Simon's Red Team to win the championship.

"I can't take a tantrum today," Mom was overheard whispering. "We're flying to New York, I have to get him on an airplane, and I just can't take it. I can't take it."

According to sources, Coach Nathaniel suggested that she drug Coach Simon with a children's Benadryl. The proposition was considered but ultimately rejected, since Coach Simon was "getting heavy," and carrying him out of LaGuardia would be "a nightmare."

Sources claim Coach Nathaniel was offered Ovaltine to throw the match. This bribe was refused, but apparently some Nutter Butters did exchange hands.

POSTGAME REPORT

In a match some foosball fans have called "a total farce," Coach Simon's Red Team defeated the Blue Team today by a score of 10–0. Rumors of corruption are rampant, with many spectators asking for a refund.

All ten goals were scored "accidentally" by members of

the Blue Team, who repeatedly kicked the ball backward, into their own net.

"You want to win," said Red Team halfback Donald Mursgard, "but not like this."

Coach Nathaniel, who openly ate Nutter Butters throughout the forty-two-second match, had no comment for reporters. Coach Simon did speak to the press for several minutes, but unfortunately, his comments were unintelligible. The conference ended with him falling down and flailing his limbs in a kind of ecstatic mania. It was around this time that Commissioner Mom offered him some Ovaltine. Coach Simon complained that the drink tasted "like medicine," but that did not stop him from consuming the whole glass and asking for seconds. As he waited for his refill, the jubilant coach fell asleep, victorious at last.

BIRTHDAY PARTY

Stephen moved to Bed-Stuy right after college, determined to make it as a writer. At first, his goal was to publish only pieces he believed in: long-form journalism, first-person essays, maybe the occasional short story. Within a year, though, it was clear that he'd set the bar too high. He owed two months of rent to his roommates, and he'd eaten so much instant ramen, he'd contracted sodium poisoning. If he wanted to survive, he had to lower his creative standards.

In his second year in Bed-Stuy, he started writing online celebrity profiles. In his third year, he moved on to celebrity listicles. In his fourth, he transitioned to recaps of reality shows. By his five-year college reunion, which he chose not to attend, he was mostly writing captions for slide shows about dogs. He was working on a long one about pugs when an email popped into his inbox. A friend from his college literary magazine had landed a gig at Zipbop.com, a "corporate branding" start-up in San Francisco. The business was expanding, and they were looking to hire "content specialists." Stephen wasn't entirely sure what all that meant, but he downloaded a résumé template, rattled something off, and within two weeks he was living in California.

Since then, his life had been a blur of sun and bliss. Each day he Ubered to his open-plan office, drank a double espresso, and went to a "dreamscaping" session, where every idea he uttered, no matter how vague, was met with respectful "hmms" by his new colleagues. He wasn't sure how his company made money or even what services they provided. But they seemed to be thriving. In his first six months on the job, he'd been to four company-mandated wine tastings. At some point, the office had hired a full-time masseuse. For Christmas, his boss gave him a mountain bike.

For the first time in memory, he was sleeping through the night without having sweat-drenched money nightmares. His student loans were paid off, and his credit score was climbing. He hadn't felt such an intense sense of relief since the summer after eighth grade, when his orthodontist had removed his orange-and-purple-colored braces.

Stephen wasn't religious, but he felt the need to say "Thank you" to the universe. And it was in this spirit of gratitude that he planned his thirtieth birthday party.

He invited the entire Zipbop family, including several bearded coders who never spoke and made him feel uncomfortable. He sprung for shrimp cocktail and Joel Gott Zinfandel. Even the cake was a crowd-pleaser—a multi-tiered sponge with creamy chocolate frosting. Pretty much the only thing he screwed up was the candles. He forgot to buy them until the last minute and had to pick some up at an odd, unmarked curio shop. The store only offered one type of candle and they didn't mesh great with the cake. They were squat, red, and engraved on all sides with screaming skeletons. Still, at least they were small. Stephen had no trouble fitting thirty of them in a circle around his name.

"Happy birthday, dear Steph-ennnnn…happy birthday to you!"

Stephen blew at the oddly shaped candles, then flushed with embarrassment. Almost half of the wicks remained lit.

"Whoops!" he said to the crowd. He was about to blow out the rest when something strange occurred to him.

Time, it seemed, had stopped.

Stephen's guests were frozen where they stood, like wax-museum versions of themselves. Their limbs were stiff and posed, their eyes cold and unblinking. One of the bearded coders was frozen in the middle of spilling his drink. A few drops of vodka hung beside his wrist, suspended in the air like floating beads of glass.

The only thing moving was a skinny, slouched kid on the other side of the room. He was staring at Stephen from inside a bright blue sphere that resembled a giant soap bubble.

Stephen put on his glasses and studied the boy as he stepped out of the orb. He was too young to be on the guest list, but everything about him looked familiar: the Sex Pistols tee shirt, the half-dyed spiky hair, the orange-and-purple-colored braces.

Stephen glanced at his cake and counted the candles he'd failed to blow out: fourteen. He felt a chill down his back. Of course—the kid walking toward him was fourteen on the dot. Stephen remembered that birthday clearly. His mother had begged him to change out of his Sex Pistols tee shirt before Grandma saw it. He'd refused, insisting that she "see the truth."

"What's going on?" the kid asked.

"It's my thirtieth birthday party," Stephen responded shyly. "Or, I guess, *our* thirtieth birthday party!"

He laughed good-naturedly. His fourteen-year-old self did not join in.

Stephen sat with his teenage self on a couch and tried his best to explain his present circumstances.

"I'm not sure why it's called Zipbop," he admitted, "but it's a great place to work. You're going to love it, Stephen!"

"It's Spike," murmured his younger self.

"Oh, right," Stephen said, remembering the self-selected nickname. He'd spent eighth grade trying to popularize it, but it hadn't come close to catching on. "So, *Spike*," he continued politely, "do you have any questions for me?"

Spike shrugged. "I guess I kind of want to know, like, how does it feel?"

"Being successful?"

"No," Spike said. "Sucking the Man's *dick*."

Stephen sighed. This was the reaction he had feared.

"I don't think that's a fair assessment of my life," he told the teenager.

"You were supposed to be a writer," Spike reminded him.

He was going through puberty, and his voice was bizarre— strong but adenoidal, sort of like the mayor of Munchkin- land.

"I *am* a writer," Stephen reminded the boy. "That's what 'content specialist' means. We went over this at length."

"You were supposed to write *experimental protest novels* that *changed the world*. Not bullshit fucking *advertisements*."

Stephen forced a smile. He could feel his patience waning.

"Okay, for starters, we don't use the *A* word at Zipbop. It's corporate messaging. And also, my job is way more cre- ative than you think. That's our company's entire mission statement—to come up with creative solutions."

"Yeah, creative solutions for how to suck on the Man's dick."

"Are you finished?"

Spike shrugged.

"Okay, listen," Stephen said, adopting a firm, almost fatherly tone. "This isn't going to be easy to hear. But the reason we're not a writer is because we're not very good at writing."

Spike folded his bony arms. "What do you mean?"

"I'll show you," Stephen said. He took out his iPhone.

"Whoa," Spike said. "Is that a computer?"

"No, it's a phone, but there's, like, internet on it."

"That's pretty cool," Spike said begrudgingly.

Stephen nodded. "Yeah, it's cool. So anyway, check it out. Here's our senior fiction thesis."

He handed the phone to Spike.

"Why are there so many footnotes?" asked the kid.

"I was trying to rip off this writer named David Foster Wallace. You'll read him next year."

"This sucks," Spike said.

"Exactly," Stephen said. He gestured around the room. "Spike, look, I know this isn't where we thought we'd end up. But it's pretty damn good. So what do you say? Can you let me off the hook?"

The teen folded his arms and cocked his head. His bottom braces were clogged with Doritos, and a few scraggly hairs protruded from the bottom of his chin, giving him the appearance of a young goat.

"No," he spat. He clumsily scrolled through the iPhone, jabbing the screen at random.

"What are you doing?" Stephen asked.

"Looking for a calculator."

"Pulling up calculator," Siri said.

"Whoa," Spike said, jerking back a little. "Sick." He wriggled his shoulders, shaking off his awe. "Okay, so anyway, check it out. How much does rent cost in whatever year this is? Not in a fancy yuppie place. Just, like, the *basics*."

Stephen hesitated. He could sense where the fourteen-year-old was going.

"How much per month?" Spike demanded. "Like, two hundred bucks?"

"More like two thousand."

"Fine," Spike said. He typed in the numbers. "Okay, so that's rent, and then you add some cash for food and stuff and multiply by twelve." He tilted the phone toward Stephen. "Do you have this much saved up?"

"I mean, yes, technically," Stephen admitted. "Maybe a little less after this party."

"Then quit your job and devote a year to writing. That's so much time! You could write an entire fucking novel!"

Stephen laughed. "I don't even have an idea for a novel."

"Yes, you do," Spike said. He reached into his pocket and pulled out a worn moleskin. Stephen felt the hairs on his neck stand up. He hadn't thought about that small black book in years, but at one point it had been his most cherished possession.

"This thing is full of book ideas," Spike said.

Stephen folded his arms. "Then why don't *you* write them?"

"Because I don't have time, remember? Biology's kicking my ass. Mom's riding my nuts about Hebrew school confirmation. I can barely take a shit without her yelling at me to practice the goddamn fucking cello." He pointed a grimy finger at Stephen's face. "But you don't have any excuses. You're a grown-up! Nobody's telling you what to do! You can drop everything, right now, and follow our dreams!"

Stephen stood up. "That's insane."

"No, it's not!" Spike said. He leapt to his feet and brandished the moleskin at Stephen, backing him slowly across the frozen room. "It's not too late! Please! You can't give up!"

Stephen bumped into something; he turned and saw that

31

they'd drifted all the way back to the cake table. The four-teen candles were still blazing.

"Just leave me alone," Stephen pleaded. "I'm happy here."

"I don't believe you!" Spike said. He whipped the mole-skin against Stephen's chest. There was a whooshing sound as the book cut through the air—and extinguished all but seven of the candles.

Spike and Stephen shared a nervous glance as a bluish bubble formed across the room. A little boy was stepping out of it. He wore new Velcro sneakers and a plastic birth-day crown from Chuck E. Cheese's.

"I remember that party," Stephen said softly.

Spike swallowed. "Me too."

They made their way over to the seven-year-old and crouched down to eye level.

"Hi, Stephen," Stephen said.

"It's Steve," said the seven-year-old.

Steve was pretty frightened when his older selves explained the situation to him—how he had been transported from his seventh birthday party to his thirtieth through some form of candle-based curse. He calmed down, though, when they said he could have Sprite.

Stephen and Spike made their cases to the boy, arguing the merits and drawbacks of working for Zipbop.com. They hadn't explicitly stated it, but it was understood that the seven-year-old would serve as the tiebreaker. It was a lot of power to give to a small child, but somehow it seemed to be the only way to settle the debate.

"So what do you think?" Spike said. "Should he stay at this dumb job or quit to be a writer?"

"That's leading him," Stephen snapped. He smiled warmly at the boy. "Steve, there's no wrong answer. I mean, yeah, the Zipbop office has a refrigerator full of Sprite, and you can drink all the Sprite you want all day..."

Spike punched Stephen in the arm.

"Just tell us who you think is right," Spike pleaded. "Me or him."

The seven-year-old finished the last of his soda and let out a satisfied belch.

"Advertising's stupid," he said.

Spike raised his scrawny arms in triumph.

"We should be doing our dream," said the seven-year-old. "Basketball."

Spike slowly lowered his arms. "What?"

"We should be playing for the Knicks," Steve said. "Or, second choice, Sonics."

"That's insane," Spike said. "We're way too short to play in the NBA." He gestured at Stephen. "I mean, look, this is us at thirty. He's, like, one of the shortest guys in this room. He's shorter than some of the women."

"He's taller than Muggsy Bogues!" Steve said. The Sprite had entered his bloodstream, making him slightly twitchy. "He's taller than Bogues, and Bogues made it to the NBA because he had a dream and he believed in himself!"

"Muggsy Bogues can jump, like, four feet in the air," Spike pointed out.

"We can get taller!" Steve insisted. There was a desperate look in his eyes. "If we hang on the monkey bars, we can get taller!"

"That doesn't work," Spike said.

"Oh God!" moaned the boy. "Oh *God!*"

Stephen shot Spike a smug smile. "See?" he said. "If anything, we're supposed to be pursuing basketball."

Spike shook his head with frustration. "This kid doesn't know what he's talking about. Writing has always been our dream. Basketball is just a phase we went through because Mom bought us NBA Jam."

"That's not true!" Steve cried.

"Yes, it is!" Spike said. "We wanted to write our whole lives, since the very beginning!" His eyes narrowed. "I'll prove it to you."

Steve and Stephen watched with concern as Spike ran over to the cake.

"Be careful!" Stephen cautioned. But it was too late. Spike had already blown out five more candles. A bluish bubble appeared on the opposite side of the room. It was smaller than the previous bubbles, about the size of a beach ball. There was a long pause, and then a toddler tottered out, his face a mask of terror.

"It's okay!" Spike said, waving to the little boy. "You're safe, Steve."

"It's Stevie," said the toddler.

Stephen couldn't help but smile at the sight of his two-year-old self. His face was smeared with frosting from his second birthday party. Something involving balloon animals, if he remembered the photographs correctly.

Spike gestured at the toddler. "We're not going to get a purer version of ourselves. So whatever he says, goes. Deal?"

Steve and Stephen nodded. "Deal," they both said.

Spike sat down cross-legged on the floor and smiled at the two-year-old.

"Stevie, listen to me," he said. "I need you to concentrate. What do you want to be when you grow up?"

The toddler looked up at the ceiling, his attention span already waning.

"Stevie, please, this is important. If you could be anything in the world, what would it be?"

It wasn't easy, but eventually Stevie was able to formulate an answer.

"Basketball."

The seven-year-old pumped his fist in the air. "I told you guys!"

He ran over to the two-year-old and gave him a hug. "Good job, Stevie!"

The two-year-old grinned, basking in the big boy's praise. "Basketball!" he repeated. "Big orange ball. And they dunk us."

"Wait, wait, wait," Stephen said. "Hold on. Wait." He knelt down and smiled gently at the two-year-old. "Stevie, is your dream to *play* basketball when you grow up? Or is it to somehow, like, physically *become* a basketball?"

The toddler thought hard for a beat. "Become basketball," he said firmly.

"That's not possible," Spike said with frustration. "You're a human being. You can't turn into a ball. That's retarded."

The two-year-old burst into tears.

"This sucks," Spike said. His other selves nodded in agreement.

"I've got an idea," Stephen said eventually. "Spike, you've got that stupid Zippo, right? With the anarchy sticker?"

"It's not stupid; it's hard-core."

"Whatever, just give it to me."

Spike handed him his lighter. Stephen walked to the cake and nervously relit one of the candles. The moment it ignited, the two-year-old vanished. Stephen exhaled with relief and lit some more candles—a fourth, a fifth, a sixth, a seventh. When he lit the eighth candle, the seven-year-old disappeared as well. He was almost up to number fifteen when Spike held up his hands.

"Whoa, hold on!" Spike said. "How do we know this is safe?"

"I'm sure it's fine," Stephen said. "You probably just go back to your own time."

He moved the lighter closer to the cake.

"Wait!" Spike pleaded. "Before you vanish me, can I, like..."

"What?" Stephen asked.

Spike shook his head and shrugged. "Never mind. It's fine."

"What?" Stephen asked, genuinely curious. "What were you going to say?"

Spike's pimply face reddened. "I was just going to ask, like, would it be okay if I..." He gestured vaguely at the frozen party guests.

"If you *what*?" Stephen demanded.

Spike looked down at the floor. "Touched some boobs."

"No!" Stephen said.

"Okay!" Spike said, throwing up his hands with embarrassment. "I'm sorry! It was just a question!"

"That's assault," said the thirty-year-old. "That's the *definition* of assault."

"Okay! Jesus! I'm sorry."

There was a long, awkward pause.

"So that's a hard 'No'?" Spike asked softly.

"Yes!"

"Okay." Spike turned away from Stephen. "Just vanish me," he murmured, ashamed. "Vanish me, vanish me."

Stephen lit the fifteenth candle, and the teenager mercifully disappeared. Stephen was overjoyed until he noticed something strange.

He appeared to be standing inside a large blue bubble.

Stephen took a deep breath and nervously stepped out of the thin, translucent orb. There was a giant cake set up on a table. It had seventy squat red candles on it—thirty of them still burning.

An old man wheeled toward him on a swift, motorized cart. "I knew those damn candles looked familiar," he said. He smiled at Stephen and thrust out a liver-spotted hand. "Welcome to your seventieth birthday, Corporal."

Stephen's eyes widened. "Corporal?"

"Oh, right," said his older self. "You're from before the war."

Stephen noticed a flag on the wall, featuring a robot holding up a knife.

"I imagine you have some questions about the flag," said his older self.

Stephen nodded.

"It's complicated," said the seventy-year-old. "But basically, it's humans versus robots now. I mean, that's, like, the CliffsNotes version? But, you know, that's more or less the situation."

"Wow," Stephen said. "What's it like fighting robots all the time?"

The old man hung his head. "I'm actually a traitor," he admitted. "I work for the robots, helping them find kids to eat."

"The robots eat kids?"

"Yep, they eat their brains. Their heads are, like, eggs to them."

"Jesus."

The old man peered up nervously at Stephen. "I bet you're disappointed, huh? In how we turn out?"

Stephen thought about it for a moment. "I mean, I'm definitely *surprised*," he said. "But I don't know. I guess the main thing is...are you happy?"

The corporal's expression brightened. "I am," he said. "I mean, my job's not perfect. But I've got a ton of friends. A beautiful robot wife. Three incredible half-robot kids."

"Kids? How does that work?"

"It's complicated," the old man admitted.

"Does your robot wife ever try to eat your kids?"

"It's complicated," he said again. "But, you know, we get through it."

Stephen nodded. "It sounds to me like you're doing everything right."

The old man smiled with relief. "I'm trying my best," he said.

Stephen threw his arms around the old man's body. "I'm proud of you," he said, giving him a tender squeeze.

"You too," said the old man.

Stephen handed the corporal the Zippo and saluted as the old man lit the candles. There was a bright blue flash and then he was back in the present, back where he belonged.

THE BOOK OF SIMON

Now, there was a righteous Hebrew in the land of Uz named Job. And no one had more faith in God than he did. And God would often boast about this man, who worshipped Him with all his heart.

But Satan said unto the Lord, "Job only praises you because his life is blessed." So God made a wager with Satan: "Destroy all that Job has, and you will see he still believes." So Satan rained horror upon Job, killing his livestock and marring his flesh with boils. And behold, the righteous Hebrew still praised God.

Over the course of the next four thousand years, the Hebrews became less religious. They ceased to make burnt offerings to God. They still had bar mitzvahs, but these were mainly just excuses to throw parties. Sometimes the bar mitzvahs would even have a nonreligious theme, like "Broadway" or "New York Sports Teams," and every table would tie into the theme. So, for example, if the theme was "Broadway," the tables would say THE LION KING or MAMMA MIA! and have decorations on them that had to do with those shows. And parents would hire professional dancers to come and teach the children dances, which were often sexually suggestive. And if there were older teenagers present, they would steal drinks from the grown-ups and get wasted on a level that was really crazy, like a "Where's the closest hospital?" kind of situation.

So Satan, who loved to gloat, started hanging out on God's cloud all the time. And he would point to the bar mitzvah parties and the empty synagogues and the latest Bill Maher YouTube clips. And he would say things like "What's up now?" or even, more aggressively, "'Sup now?" And by the twenty-first century, God's self-esteem was at an all-time low.

Now, there was a wicked Hebrew in the land of Brooklyn named Simon Rich. And no one had less faith in God than he. And Satan would often boast about this man.

But God said unto Satan, "Maybe Simon would believe in me if his life were more blessed?" And Satan laughed and said, "How?" For Simon had been raised in luxury and had never experienced hardship of any kind.

So God, whose back was to the wall, made a wager with Satan. "Let's go double or nothing on the Job thing. I'll bless Simon and give him reward upon reward, until his cup runneth over. And you will see that he starts to believe!" And God put everything aside, including Africa, and focused full-time on blessing this Jewish atheist.

Now, Simon had graduated from an expensive college, but he had almost no skills. All he liked to do was sit around in his underwear, making up jokes and then laughing at them. So God said, "Fine," and let Simon do that as his full-time job. But instead of praising God for this miracle, Simon took everything for granted and even began to write some jokes that made fun of God. And Satan would read these jokes out loud to God, in an irritating voice. And although the Lord was angered, He was not yet prepared to admit defeat. "I will give Simon even more blessings," He vowed. "And sooner or later, he will become a believer."

So the Lord continued to bless the screenwriter with health and wealth and unfair tax breaks, which Simon claimed to be against politically but secretly voted for in every election. And then there came a day when Simon fell in love with a beautiful Christian woman. And Satan nudged God and said, "Now what?" And God let out a heavy groan and cried, "Has anyone ever been tested such as me?" And Job shot God an annoyed look. And God was embarrassed because He had not seen that Job was standing on the cloud with them. So He awkwardly led Satan over to a different cloud. And then He warped time and space so that Simon could date this pretty shiksa. And by this time things in Africa were getting really bad. And even Satan was like, "Shouldn't you get on that?" But God was fixated on this Simon thing.

Soon it came time for Simon's wedding. And Simon's mother asked him if he wanted a Jewish ceremony. And God scooted forward to the edge of His cloud, anxious to see how Simon would respond. And Simon said that he would have to think about it.

And that night, for the first time since his *Simpsons*-themed bar mitzvah, Simon wrestled deeply with his faith. He thought about all of the blessings he'd been given while other, more deserving people starved and died. And the mad injustice of his life convinced him, unequivocally, that God could not exist. Because if God existed, then surely by now he would have gotten some horrible comeuppance.

So Simon told his mom that he didn't want a Jewish ceremony but also that he didn't really care, and that he would go through the motions if the thing was really short and she paid for it all. And after the wedding, at which pork was served, God gave Satan fifty bucks and said, "You win." And Satan tried to gloat, but he couldn't enjoy the victory, because God was so visibly upset. So he turned to the Lord with pity and said, "I'll tell you what. Someday soon I'll make Simon believe. I'll give him that proof that he's been waiting for."

And God said, "What are you going to do to him?"

And Satan grinned and said, "You'll see."

RELAPSE

Zoe still got recognized sometimes. She'd be walking with Tom through the farmers' market, pushing Alice in the stroller, and a tattooed person (they were usually tattooed people) would point at her and say, "Are you who I think you are?"

"Maybe!" was Zoe's standard response. "I used to be in a band?"

"Yes!" the fan would say. And they would recite her band's name, in a proud tone of voice, like a confident contestant on *Jeopardy!* "That's the one!" Zoe would say. At this point the fan would almost always walk away. Sometimes, though, they would make Zoe's day by complimenting one of her songs. It was usually her only hit—the single from her first album that had somehow made it onto MTV. Occasionally, though, they brought up an obscure track, something she hadn't thought about in years, and all at once, the song would come to her, the lyrics, chords, and harmonies, and her eyes would glaze over, and her mind would flash back to the place where she had been when she wrote it, a squeaky bed in Amsterdam, on exotic hotel stationery, next to a smelly but sexy foreign club promoter, or on a tour bus somewhere in Nebraska, squinting at her notepad in the moonlight, her body still tingling from the rush of a solid, sold-out gig. Then Tom would make his joke about how the fan should buy the song on iTunes so they could get eight cents, and Alice would flail in her stroller, as if aware and offended that her mother had been thinking about the past, about the era that predated her birth, and Zoe would snap back to the present. "It was nice meeting you," she would say. And after a handshake (her fans were too old for selfies), she would shoot Tom an eye roll, to conceal the thrill these encounters secretly gave her, and they would walk in silence to the parking lot and load all their shit into the Prius.

Quitting music had been a gradual thing, so gradual that Zoe had barely realized that she was doing it.

When she first met Tom, they were both professional artists. It was at a New Year's party in the hills thrown by some movie producer. She was there because the producer had used her MTV song in a soundtrack. Tom was there because the producer had optioned the film rights to one of his short stories. She remembered how he had looked at that party—his bangs flopping over his mischievous eyes, his boyish cheeks reddened by booze. When she asked him about his film deal, he spoke about it with convincing ambivalence. He was sure the movie would be bad, but he needed the money to pay the rent while he finished his first novel. They had sex upstairs, in some kind of storage room, surrounded by bubble-wrapped art prints that had come back from the framer's but hadn't yet been mounted on the walls. While Tom was fucking her, Zoe realized with shock that her song had started playing on the stereo downstairs. She came during the final chorus, while listening to her own disembodied voice.

The producer never adapted Tom's story, and his novel was rejected by his publisher. He started writing press releases for a PR firm, ironically at first, then after a pay raise, in earnest. Zoe hung on to her passion a bit longer, releasing a politely received second record, then a poorly received third. Venues got smaller, band members quit, and CDs became an obsolete technology. Still, Zoe kept at it, tramping through Europe doing solo acoustic sets, opening for people half her age. One day she called Tom with a phone card from a soggy field in Leipzig, after playing an outdoor show for seven teenagers, one of whom had been so drunk on vodka that she had worried he was going to die. It was 5 a.m. in California, and she didn't expect Tom to pick up the phone, but he answered on the very first ring, and the crackly sound of his voice brought her to tears.

Within a year of this rock-bottom moment, Alice was born, named after Alice Cooper but also Tom's maternal grandmother, Alice Fishbein. Zoe threw herself into parenting, secretly relieved at having an excuse to not write songs for a while or give morning FM radio interviews or play humiliating, barely attended "concerts." When Alice turned two, Zoe's friend Rusty invited her to open for him on a twelve-city tour. Although she was tempted, the fact was she couldn't justify the cost. Between gas and motels, she would barely break even. And when they added the cost of childcare, the trip became downright decadent. They were living entirely off Tom's salary by this point, and Zoe was too ashamed to ask him to fund what amounted to rock-and-roll fantasy camp. She turned down Rusty over email, too sad to say the truth out loud—that she was done, really done, with all of it.

When Alice turned three, they bought a house in Silver Lake so they could be in the Ivanhoe school district. Their friends were all recovered artists of some kind, former aspiring actors or directors who had quit their selfish dreams to embrace the realities of adulthood. Their closest confidants were Andy and Jeff, two singers turned Realtors who lived down the street and had adopted a Korean girl exactly Alice's age. Sometimes at dinner, after a few bottles of Pinot, they would talk about people like Rusty—people who were "still out there." There was Tom's old roommate Vincent, an experimental filmmaker, whose last four shorts had a combined one thousand views on YouTube. And Andy's sister, Melissa, who had gone from minor roles in major films to minor roles in minor films to actual, full-on pornography. Zoe pitied these people. And when she looked around her home, at her balding but still handsome husband and her generic but tasteful West Elm couch, she thanked the universe that she had been spared such a fate.

She was absorbed in these sorts of thoughts one night when she began to hum a melody—a taut loop of notes that felt both familiar and strange. She knew it was something she had written, but somehow she couldn't remember the name of the song. It took her a while to figure out why.

It was a new one.

Zoe was rummaging through the closet when she felt a forceful tap on her thigh. She turned and saw her five-year-old daughter, Alice, glaring up at her, her tiny arms folded across her tutu.

"We were playing balloons," Alice said.

"We're *still* playing balloons," Zoe assured her. "But how about this? Instead of throwing the deflated balloon back and forth to each other, like we've been doing for the last several hours, why don't *you* take the balloon into the living room, by yourself, and see how many times you can throw it in the air and catch it?"

Alice squinted at her mother, considering the rule change.

"I bet you can't do a hundred," Zoe said. "No one has *ever* done a hundred before. If you do a hundred, that means you're the best."

Alice grinned, taking the bait. Zoe sighed with relief as her daughter picked up the balloon and ran into the living room, screaming with moronic determination.

"One toss! Two tosses!"

Zoe turned her attention back to the closet. It wasn't easy, but eventually, under a hideous Moana blanket, she found it: the piano.

It wasn't a real piano of course—just a Fisher-Price toy an uncle had given Alice for Christmas. Still, it had twelve keys—a full octave of notes—and thanks to Alice's apathy toward music, it was in excellent condition.

Zoe placed the toy on the rug and tenderly stroked the row of plastic keys. Her Les Paul was somewhere in the basement, behind Tom's abandoned cardio machines. But she didn't need a guitar. Every melody on earth was composed of the same twelve notes. With twelve notes you could make anything you wanted.

"Sixty-three tosses...sixty-four tosses..."

There wasn't a lot of time. Zoe hummed the first note of her melody and flicked her way up the piano, tapping each key until she found the corresponding tone.

E.

From there it was simple to map out the rest of the line— a descending streak of notes, winding down the A major scale.

"Eighty-one...eighty-two..."

She could hear the rest of the song now. A minor-key bridge and some grungy, power-chord-y sort of outro. She sang out the melody, throwing in some I's and you's, the embryonic kernels of what might become the lyrics. It was a confrontational song, aggressive, but triumphant. An anthem.

"What are you doing?"

Zoe turned around and swallowed. At some point Tom had entered the room.

"Just playing with Alice," she said, casually flicking her wrist. "She wanted to try the piano."

"No, I didn't," Alice said, emerging from behind her father's legs. Her deflated balloon had lost more air during her tosses. She cradled the limp sack in her arm like a wounded animal.

"We were playing balloons," Alice said. "And then *you* sent me away so *you* could do piano. Alone."

Zoe forced a laugh. "She's just joking," she said. "Right, munchkin?"

"No," Alice said.

There was a long pause. Zoe forced a tight smile. "I've gotta pick up the groceries," she said.

Zoe drove past the Whole Foods and kept on going until she was deep in Echo Park. Rusty was waiting for her in his junk-strewn yard, acoustic guitar in hand.

"Got your text," he said. "Let's hear it."

Zoe grabbed his Yamaha by the neck and launched right into it.

"Holy shit," said Rusty, after Zoe finished up the outro.

Her face lit up. "You like it?"

"I fucking love it," he said.

Zoe laughed and threw her arms around her bony stoner friend. It had been a couple of years since she'd last seen him, and it wasn't until now that she realized how much she missed his company.

"Who's your manager?" Rusty asked her.

Zoe shrugged. "He quit the industry, like, twenty million years ago."

"Well, shit. You're going to need someone to rep you," Rusty said. "You've got a hit on your hands."

Zoe could feel her heart pounding in her chest.

"I know someone," Rusty said. He grabbed a pizza delivery menu off the ground, took out a Sharpie, and scrawled down an address. "I'll set the whole thing up," he said. "How's one p.m. Friday?"

Zoe searched her brain for prior commitments. Alice had some kind of bullshit on Friday. But she had some kind of bullshit every day. If she waited for a day when Alice didn't have some kind of bullshit, she'd be waiting for the rest of her life.

"I'll be there," she said.

She was pulling into her driveway when she realized she hadn't picked up any groceries. *Fuck it*, she thought. *Fuck it all.*

The manager lived in Hollywood, in the shadow of the Capitol Records building. She double-checked the address and knocked on the door.

"Is that Zoe?" asked an older man's voice.

"Yeah!"

"It's open. Come on in."

Zoe took a deep breath and entered the house. She'd put some thought into her outfit, settling finally on a blue velvet blazer and her Dinosaur Jr. tee shirt. She'd also brought along a rough demo she'd made of her song. She was making sure her name was spelled correctly on the jewel case when she heard her husband's voice.

"Hi, honey."

Zoe looked up and swallowed. The living room was full of familiar faces: Tom, their neighbors, Andy and Jeff, and Rusty.

"What is this?" she said. "What's going on?"

A tanned man in a sweater stepped out from the shadows.

"My name is Dr. Jenson," he said gently. "It's great to finally meet you."

He thrust out his hand. Zoe shook it awkwardly. "Are you the manager?"

He smiled sympathetically at her. "I'm sorry we misled you," he said. "It was the only way to get you here."

Zoe looked around in a panic. "What the hell is going on?"

"I know this all must be confusing," Dr. Jenson said. "But it's actually very simple. The people in this room love you like crazy. But they're scared to death of losing you. And that's why we're here."

Zoe felt her knees grow weak.

"This is an intervention?"

"We know you've been making art again," Tom said. "We know about the song. We know everything."

Zoe glared at Rusty. He stared down at his lap, too ashamed to make eye contact. "I'm sorry," he murmured. "I had to tell them."

"This is crazy!" Zoe said. "Why do you care if I start writing music again?"

"We just don't want you to get hurt," Tom said.

"Is it that?" Zoe said. "Or is it that you're fucking jealous?"

Dr. Jenson smiled patiently. "Why would they be jealous?" he asked.

"Because they're fucking failures!" Zoe said. "Tom, your novel sucked ass. It made no sense!" She turned to Jeff and Andy. "And you guys, I looked up that show you said you met in, and it wasn't even a real show! It was a Broadway-themed restaurant! You weren't singers; you were *waiters*!" She slammed her demo down on the table. "I've got something going here, and I'm not going to let you drag me down."

"You've been down this road before," said Dr. Jenson. "Tom told me about the dark days. Playing in a field somewhere, miles away from your family."

"That was different," Zoe said. "It won't end that way this time."

"It always ends that way," said Dr. Jenson.

"Look," Andy said. "Everyone dabbles with art in their twenties. You write, you act, you direct. You try it all. But it's not sustainable."

"What about Jeff?" Zoe snapped. "He still sings."

"Jeff can control it," Andy said. "He does karaoke once a week, and he's satisfied. Some people are like that. You're not."

Zoe turned to Rusty. "Dude, come on," she begged. "You know in your heart this is bullshit. Let's get out of here. You can open for me on tour—I'll let you do a folk set!"

Rusty shook his head stiffly. "I can't."

"Why not?" Zoe demanded.

Dr. Jenson placed a palm on Rusty's shoulder. "Do you want to tell Zoe your news?"

Rusty reluctantly looked up at Zoe. His eyes were damp with tears.

"I'm getting help," he murmured.

"What?" Zoe whispered.

"I can't do it anymore," he said. "The shitty tour buses. The sad motels. I'm going to New Horizons in Tampa."

He handed Zoe a brochure, and she shakily flipped through the pages.

"It's a treatment center for artists," Dr. Jenson explained. "One of the best in the world. They make it easy for you to quit. They'll prescribe wine, so you can control the cravings. After ninety days, you'll come back here and be yourself again. A friend, a wife, a mother."

"I can be all those things and make art at the same time."

Dr. Jenson nodded at Tom. He exited the room and returned moments later, holding Alice in his arms.

Zoe shook her head bitterly as Tom cajoled their daughter into speaking.

"Go ahead, munchkin," he said in a saccharine tone. "Tell your mommy what you wanted to say."

Alice looked into her mother's eyes. Her voice was unusually loud and sounded well rehearsed. "We used to play balloons. Now that you're doing art again, we don't have time to do balloons."

"Good job!" Tom said. "That was very brave!" Alice flashed her mother a smug look as her father covered her with kisses.

"That's it?" Zoe said. "I have to quit making art because she misses her goddamn balloons?"

"It's not just that," Tom said. "One time you were so busy writing a song, you left her alone with a balloon. What if she had choked on it? Huh? What then?"

Zoe's skin burned with guilt. "Okay, how about this?" she said. "I'll self-release one EP, see what Pitchfork says, and then I'll quit."

"Honey, we're past the point of bargaining," Tom said. "If you don't take the help being offered today, it's over."

Zoe's face turned pale. She felt like she was going to throw up.

"Look," Dr. Jenson said. "I know what you're going through."

"How could you possibly know?" Zoe said.

"Because I spent ten years writing poetry."

Zoe raised her eyebrows. Poetry was the nastiest addiction of them all. She couldn't help but be a little impressed.

"I got an MFA and everything," he continued. "I was ninety-five thousand dollars in debt. I was mailing submissions to *Ploughshares* once a month." He shuddered slightly at the memory. "By the end, it got so bad, I was doing open mics. And sometimes the guy before me would be a stand-up comedian. So when I came out and read my poems, people would laugh, thinking I was making some kind of weird joke. And I'd have to be like, 'No. Stop laughing. This is a poem I wrote. It's supposed to be serious.'"

"Holy shit," said Zoe.

"I thought I was going to die," said Dr. Jenson. "But then, one day, I made the decision to change. I threw out all my journals, unsubscribed to *Granta*. And now, ten years later, I've got it all. A house in Silver Lake..." He thought for a beat. "A house in Silver Lake," he repeated.

"Don't you miss it?" Zoe asked. "Writing poems?"

Dr. Jenson smiled. "Every day," he said. "But there're things you can do to dull the urges. For example, I do drugs. Every day, I take, like, a ton of painkillers." He took a white pill out of his pocket and ate it. "That was a painkiller," he told the group. "A big one."

Tom took his wife's hand. "Think about how nice it'll be," he said. "To not have to always be jonesing for hits and applause. To give up that search and just...*be.*"

Zoe felt her mouth go dry.

She loved the highs of making music, but could she still handle the lows?

What if she made a record and it flopped as badly as her last two? She imagined herself in a silent bar in Phoenix, manning a merch table heaped with ugly posters of her face. She pictured herself in New York City, peeking through a crack in the curtains, trying to work up the courage to play to a giant empty room. She'd crashed before and lived to tell the tale. But that was years ago. At this age, she might not survive it.

Zoe flipped through the brochure again. She noticed this time that the place had a pool.

"How would it work?" she asked softly. "Would I have to quit all at once?"

"No," Tom said. "They'll taper you off. The first week, they'll let you play covers, as long as you don't do anything creative, like add a solo or whatever."

"It does look kinda nice," Zoe admitted.

"Is that a yes?" asked Dr. Jenson.

"Yes," Zoe murmured.

"You know what that means!" Dr. Jenson told the group. "Time for hugs!"

Tom and Alice shared a quick victorious look, then ran up to Zoe and tightly wrapped their arms around her neck.

Tom and Alice visited Tampa sixty days in and were amazed by Zoe's progress. She was significantly calmer and way less inclined to have creative thoughts. She'd also undergone a dramatic physical transformation. The doctors had prescribed her rosé, and the sugary wine had helped her to gain fifteen pounds of fat. The extra-small Dinosaur Jr. shirt was gone, and in its place she wore a tasteful cardigan. She still had a Misfits tattoo on her ankle. That would never go away. But for the first time in her life, she looked less like a rock star than a mom.

Zoe led her family through the grounds, to the modest room she shared with a recovering photographer.

"This is where Mommy sleeps," she said to Alice. "There's my bureau, where I keep my cardigans. There's my phone, where I call you to say good night. And this is where I journal."

Tom and Alice shared a look.

"They let you journal?" Tom asked.

"It's not creative," Zoe assured him. "Sit down. I'll read you some."

Tom and Alice sat down on the bed and watched skeptically as Zoe cracked open her notebook.

"Okay," she said. "This entry is from earlier this week." She drank some rosé and read it out loud to them. "'Whole Foods grocery list: pasta, pesto, arugula, balsamic vinegar, that olive spread they have, tomatoes, rosé.'"

Tom and Alice grinned ecstatically.

"That was great!" Tom said.

"Really?" Zoe asked earnestly. "You liked it?"

"We loved it, Mommy!"

They broke into applause and wouldn't stop until she bowed to them.

HANDS

When I first came to the desert, I could tell the other monks didn't respect me. They took one look at me and thought, *That guy's not going to last out here. He's going to sin the first chance he gets.*

I didn't pay much attention to them. To be honest, I don't really care what other people have to say about me. If I cared about other people's opinions, I never would have left Babylon in the first place, and I certainly wouldn't have decided to cut off my hands.

I remember telling the monks about my choice. We were kneeling by the swamp. We had been fasting for five days, and on the third day we had each eaten a handful of salt to further heighten our agony. I could tell by the other monks' groans that they were nearing their breaking point. But I was just getting started.

"When this fast is over," I told them, "I am going to cut off my hands. Both of them. With a sword."

The eldest monk, Dominic, was the first to respond.

"That is crazy," he said. "You need your hands to do so many things."

"To do *what* things?" I challenged. "To weave baskets and other material possessions that the devil makes us covet? To feed myself food and break the holy fast? To commit sin with my *genitals*?"

While I was saying all this, I was punching myself in the face, to cancel out the sin of speech.

"Tomorrow morning," I declared, "I will go to the mountaintop and cut off both my hands. And that's final!"

The monks pulled at their beards and scratched their ribs. They didn't know what to say. I was new to the desert, but already I had risen high above them. There was nobody humbler; it wasn't even close.

"Please do not do this," Dominic said. "You will suffer so horribly."

"It will be nothing compared to the suffering of Christ," I reminded him. I was standing naked on the mountain, sharpening my blade against a rock.

"Why don't you do another fast?" Dominic tried. "Or maybe carve a cross into your chest, like Mordecai?"

I took a long, slow breath. Mordecai is a total hack. Whenever pilgrims visit our camp, he is always at the center of the clearing, "coincidentally" whipping himself at that exact moment. "Oh wow!" they say as they pass him. "What a holy monk!" Mordecai pretends not to hear them, like he's so engrossed in whipping himself that he isn't even aware of their presence. But as soon as they leave, the smugness returns to his face and his whipping comes to a stop.

"I suppose I could carve a cross into my chest," I said.

"And parade around, flaunting it to laypeople, trying to win their cheap praise. *Or* I could make a *real* sacrifice."

I held the blade over my head and examined it in the hot summer sun. It wasn't particularly sharp, but with enough savage hacks it would "do the trick," as they say.

"I cannot help you with this act of penance," Dominic said. "God gave you those hands, and I think you should keep them."

"I didn't expect you to help me," I said. "You are too weak and hypocritical."

After I said it, though, I realized I actually would need some assistance if I was going to cut off both my hands. I could use my right hand to cut off my left hand—but the next part would get tricky. I was trying to devise a solution to this trivial, earthly problem when my thoughts were interrupted by the gaudy blast of a horn.

I turned toward the sound and gasped. A procession of caravans appeared to be heading toward our camp. I counted over a dozen wagons—giant, horse-drawn carriages sheltered from the desert wind with silks of gold and purple.

Hallucinations are common among monks, due to our constant, gnawing hunger. So when you see something unusual, it is standard policy to check with a nearby monk to make sure it is real.

"Caravans, right?" I asked Dominic.

"Yeah," he confirmed. "I see them too."

We climbed down to a clearing so we could get an unobstructed view. I had never seen such a sickening sight. Each wagon was laden with indulgences: marble busts from Athens, bronze urns from Phoenicia, and garish idols from the wicked monkey worshippers of India.

The only empty wagon was the front one—a cushioned carriage reserved for a single individual.

I squinted at the smooth-skinned aristocrat. At first, the absence of a beard made me think it was a boy. But as the carriage drew closer, I realized I was looking at a young woman.

Her golden hair was glossy from a lifetime of decadence, and her lips were painted red, in the manner of a Moabite whore. She made no attempt to conceal the presence of her breasts. Her silk shirt clung to them, as taut as the skin of a grape.

"Let's go say hi," Dominic said.

"What about my hands?"

"You'll figure it out later."

I screamed with frustration, put away my blade, and followed the old man down the mountain.

Her name was Fabiola, and she came from Rome itself.

Her father was a consul, and for her eighteenth birthday, he'd consented to send her on a grand tour of the world's great wonders.

It was hard not to vomit as she held forth at our campfire, defiling our ears with tales of her decadent adventures. She'd knelt before the Statue of Zeus at Olympia and sketched Alexandria from the top of the legendary lighthouse. And now here she was, in the spiritual home of our faith. There could be only one reason why.

"I want to see it," she told Dominic. "The tomb of your God. Where you believe that he was resurrected."

I snorted at her predictability. Tourists never want to see the field where Jesus wept. They have no interest in the hill where he was crucified. They just want to see the happy ending.

We should be thankful, I suppose, that Jesus is even remembered by laypeople. In the three hundred years since his death, so much has been forgotten about our Messiah. Only a few written accounts of his life remain, and even among these there are numerous discrepancies. The Gospel According to John differs wildly from the Gospel According to Matthew. And neither account is as accurate as the Gospel According to Hector.

(Incidentally, Mordecai is in charge of protecting the Gospel According to Hector, and I am 90 percent sure he's lost the scroll. One time I flat-out asked him where it was. "It's in my tent," he said. So I was like, "Great. Can I see it?" And he was like, "It's under a lot of stuff." How much stuff can he possibly have? The man is a monk.)

"The path to Jesus is arduous," Dominic told Fabiola.

The girl grinned with excitement. "Is that, like, one of your monk parables?"

"No," Dominic said. "I just mean, like, getting to Jesus's tomb is a real hassle. It's a three-day climb up a mountain through all sorts of streams and thickets. There wouldn't be room for your caravans."

"That's fine," the girl said, waving her polished nails through the air. "I want the full, authentic experience. That's the whole reason I'm doing this trip. To expand my mind and see the world."

I couldn't take it anymore. I stood up, punched myself preemptively in the face, and began speaking.

"How can you 'see the world' when you are blind? Your eyes notice only that which glitters!"

I expected the girl to weep with shame, but instead she smiled and nodded.

"You seem like a pretty hard-core monk," she said. "Why don't you guide me to Jesus's tomb and, you know, explain it to me?"

"Not a chance!" I said. "Its meaning would be lost on you!"

"I'd be happy to make a donation to your group."

"How much?" Dominic asked.

"We don't accept gifts," I reminded him.

"What about grain?" said the girl. "You guys must need some grain to live out here in the desert."

"It's true that our weak mortal flesh requires grain," I admitted. "But we do not accept it as payment. We eat only food that people leave behind by accident."

"What does that mean?"

I showed her the large earthen urn that contains our communal grain supply.

"Once a year," I explained, "we go to the market and

pick up the grain that people have spilled on the dirty, filthy ground. And even *this* grain is too decadent for us. Which is why I add urine."

"You've been adding *urine*?" Dominic asked.

I nodded. "I've been adding some urine."

"Your own?"

"Yes," I said.

"To the big urn? The one we all eat out of?"

"Yes."

"Oh man," Dominic said, softly shaking his head. "Man."

There was a long silence. Eventually the girl cleared her throat.

"Listen," she said. "I totally understand that you guys don't accept gifts. Everyone has their own quirks. For example, my servants, they're really forgetful. Whenever they get distracted, they leave stuff behind." She locked eyes with Dominic. "You know...*by accident.*"

Dominic swallowed. "Explain more what you mean by that."

The girl continued, a mischievous smile on her face. "Well, for example, if they found out that I had been all the way to Jesus's tomb, the news would distract them so much I wouldn't be surprised if they *accidentally* left behind five urns of grain." She leaned toward Dominic, her dark eyes shining demonically in the fire's glow. "Five urns of urine-free grain."

Dominic gestured at me. "He'll take you."

"No I won't!" I said. "I came to the desert to purify my soul! Not to help indulge some privileged Roman whore!"

I punched myself once more in the face and then headed off into the freezing night.

"Wait," Dominic said.

I turned around. "What?"

Dominic covered his face with his palms. "I can't believe I'm saying this," he murmured. "This is so crazy." He shuddered slightly and then looked at me. "If you take this girl up the mountain...I will help you cut off your hands."

"He's going to cut off his *hands*?" the girl asked.

"Yes," Dominic said, meeting my eyes. "And when he does, the feat will make him the most respected monk in Christian history. He'll surpass everyone: Macarius the Sufferer, Palladius the Sunburnt, Pablo the Getter of the Rash."

I bowed my head, humbled to hear my name among such luminaries.

"Okay," I said. "I'm in."

I watched with impatience as the girl packed for the journey, filling up crate after crate with her extravagances.

"It must be kind of fun out here," she said. "Just camping out all day with your friends."

"I have no friends," I said.

"What about the other monks?"

"They are just that," I said. "Other monks."

She looked up from her baggage. "What about back home?"

"The desert is my home," I reminded her. "The sand is

my bed, the sky is my walls, a rock is my pillow, my hands are my toilet."

"I know, I know," she said. "I meant, like, your *home* home. Like, where you're originally from."

"Who cares where I'm originally from?"

"Come on, just tell me."

I gritted my teeth. "I was born in the city of Satan himself," I confessed. "Babylon."

"Oh cool, I love Babylon," she said. "I have camp friends from there. You ever go back?"

"Once a year."

"To visit family?"

"I will never again break bread with those idolaters!"

"So why do you go back?"

"To test myself," I explained. "Last year, for example, I went to the market and picked up a large sausage. I held it inside my open mouth and kept it there for hours. Tears of hunger streamed down my face. But I didn't take so much as a nibble. Instead, at nightfall, I placed the sausage back upon the table and drank urine."

"Where'd you get the urine?"

"I carry urine with me on these trips."

"How?"

"In a urine bag that I continually refill."

"That sounds like a pretty bad trip," she said.

"It was," I said proudly.

She added one last crate to her pile.

"Okay," she said. "I think that's everything."

She picked up the smallest of the crates. "Think you can handle the rest?"

"My condition is so weak from fasting that it hurts to even stand. Walking is agony, climbing is torture, and carrying crates would be pain beyond description."

"Isn't pain your thing?"

I averted my eyes. She had me there.

"I can probably carry two crates," I said.

"Then we're going to need more help," she said. Her eyes narrowed. "How about that whip guy?"

I turned and saw Mordecai standing right behind me, pretending not to eavesdrop.

"I am sorry for disturbing you, ma'am," he said. "I was self-flagellating, and in my meditative state, I happened to wander to this spot."

"What a coincidence!" I said facetiously. "Of all the spots in the desert you could wander to, you ended up at the one that contains a tourist!"

I rolled my eyes at Fabiola, but she did not reciprocate. She was staring at Mordecai's chest, her eyes wide with amazement.

"Whoa," she said. "Is that a *cross*?"

Mordecai looked down and shrugged. "Oh, this old thing? Yeah, it's a cross. I carved it one night in a fit of devotion." He flicked his wrist. "It's no big deal."

"Oh my Gods," she said. "I need to get a picture with you." She opened up her art chest, took out a canvas, and handed me a brush. "Do you mind painting us together?"

"No pictures!" I said. "Let's just get this stupid journey over with."

And so the three of us headed up the mountain. Mordecai had taken the lightest crates, so he could keep up with Fabiola while I fell increasingly behind. I tried not to listen as he boasted to the girl.

"Did it hurt? Well, yeah. It's a full cross. And I carved it right into my chest. But what can I say? A monk's got to do what a monk's got to do."

I clenched my jaw in stoic agony. The Lord tests me often in the desert, but nothing compares to the pain of having to listen to Mordecai, with the possible exception of sand hemorrhoids, which are pretty crazy.

"You know what I think sometimes?" Mordecai rambled. "What if none of this is real? What if we're all just, like, in some guy's dream? And if that guy woke up, we'd disappear?"

"That's not even Christianity!" I shouted. But they ignored me.

"I think about words sometimes too," Mordecai continued. "Like when you say a normal word over and over again, it starts to sound weird. Like, for example, look at the word 'word.' *Word, word, word, word, word*. It starts to sound weird, right?"

"Man," Fabiola said. "I've never thought about any of these things before. This stuff is *deep*."

"Really? You think so?"

"Big-time. I feel like I'm getting the full authentic monk experience."

She flashed a small, subtle smile over her shoulder. Was it possible she was only praising Mordecai to torture me?

We came to a sunlit clearing. "Okay!" Fabiola said, setting down her crate. "Break time."

"We're not taking a break," I said. "We've barely started climbing."

"What do you think, Mordecai?" she asked. "Should we lie down and break for a bit?"

Mordecai's face flushed. "Break sounds good," he murmured.

I shot him a disgusted look as the girl opened her crate and laid out a debauched feast: honey, breads, and three cups made of pure Anatolian silver.

"What are those for?" I asked.

"It wouldn't be a picnic without wine," she said. She pulled out a large green bottle and began to fill the cups. When she got to mine, I politely held up my hand.

"Just urine for me, thanks."

"Come on," Fabiola said. "You can have a little. Even Jesus drank wine, right?"

"I have taken a vow of ascetic devotion," I reminded her as I took out my urine bag. "I know it must shock you, but some of us value things in life beyond base pleasure."

I turned to Mordecai and saw that he had already finished his entire cup of wine. He wiped his grape-stained mouth and burped a little.

"I was going to bring urine too," he murmured to the girl, "but I was whipping myself so hard that I forgot to bring some."

I rolled my eyes and snorted.

"What?" Mordecai asked defensively.

"If you wanted to drink urine," I said, "you could easily produce some right now. Lord knows your bladder is full enough with decadent, syrupy wine!"

His face reddened. "Maybe I *will* produce urine!" he said.

"Guys, this is crazy," Fabiola said. "Nobody has to drink urine."

"She's right," I said. "Nobody has to be devout and holy. Some of us can be decadent hypocrites who are too afraid to drink their own urine."

"I'll be right back!" said Mordecai. He grabbed his empty cup and ran into the forest.

"You're way too hard on him," Fabiola said. "He's obviously incredibly insecure."

"He should be," I said. "The only reason he even got to be a monk is because he's the son of Hagaron."

"Who's Hagaron?"

I groaned into my hands, dismayed by her ignorance.

"Okay," I said. "So you know how we all walk around completely naked all the time, except for a tiny strip of fabric to cover up our penis holes?"

She nodded. "I've noticed that."

"Hagaron *invented* that. That's *his* look. We're all kind of just, like, doing variations on it."

"Huh," she said. I could tell by her tone that she didn't think Hagaron was that big of a deal.

"He was a very big deal!" I said.

"What about *your* dad?" she asked.

I choked a little on my urine. "Excuse me?"

"What does *he* do?"

"Why does it matter what he does?"

"I'm just curious," she said.

"He works for a wealthy man," I said. "You might have heard of him. His name is the *Dark Lord Lucifer*!"

There was a long pause.

"He's a merchant," I explained. "He sells silver to aristo-crats."

"That's impressive."

"Generating wealth is not impressive," I said. "Denying it is."

"Sounds like you're pretty competitive with him."

"That's absurd," I said. "I'm a monk. Monks are incapable of competitiveness."

Mordecai emerged from the forest. "Okay," he said. "I urinated in my cup, and now I'm going to drink it."

"That's not urine," I pointed out immediately. "It's water from a stream."

Mordecai's eyes darted briefly toward the girl. "It's urine!" he insisted.

"Then why are there little bits of grass in it?" I asked.

"Just leave me alone!" he said. "Leave me alone and let me drink my urine!"

I grabbed the cup from his hands and downed the liquid in a single gulp.

"It was water!" I said triumphantly. "Decadent, thirst-quenching water!"

Mordecai looked down at his feet. His face had turned redder than the desert sun.

"Now if you'll excuse me," I said, "I have to get that pleasurable taste out of my mouth."

I took out my urine bag and was about to take a sip when Mordecai ripped it from my hands.

"What are you doing?" I asked.

"I'm going to drink *your* urine!" Mordecai said.

I rolled my eyes. "I'd like to see that!"

Fabiola stepped between us. "Mordecai, this is ridiculous," she whispered to him. "You don't have to do this."

"She's right," I said. "Who cares who among us is a true servant of Christ? Who cares whose faith is real and whose is just a ploy to impress a *woman*?"

That did it. Mordecai opened the bag and poured the cloudy liquid into his gaping mouth. Fabiola turned away, disgusted, as it splashed onto his face and up his nose. When the bag was empty, he fell to his knees and slowly caught his breath.

"I need to be alone," he said eventually. "I need to find a stream and just...be alone."

I laughed as he staggered off into the brush.

Fabiola turned to me, her fair, smooth forehead crinkled with hostility. "Why did you do that to him? How could you be so cruel?"

"I was merely trying to teach you a lesson," I informed her. "You thought he was a man of God, but in fact he was a spiritual imposter!"

I picked up the bag and squeezed the remaining urine into my mouth, sucking down every last drop. I beat on my chest, to suppress my involuntary gags, then turned to the girl and nodded.

"Cool," she muttered. "You won. Congratulations."

We walked for several miles in silence. Even by monk standards, it felt like a pretty long time to go without speaking.

"Is everything all right?" I asked when we had reached the tree line. "Are we cool?"

"Yeah," she said. "We're cool."

"Cool," I said.

But I still wasn't totally sure if we were cool. It was a bizarre situation. I was a man of God. She was a demonic hedonist. And yet I couldn't help but feel like she was judging me.

I spent the next few hours trying to lighten the mood by telling her entertaining stories. Like the time when I fasted for ten days. Or the time when I fasted for twelve days. Or the time when I fasted for eight days, twice in a row, but it was really more like sixteen days because I had had only a little bit of grain between the two eight-day fasts. But somehow these tales failed to delight her. Her eyes remained glazed and her expression cold and grim. She didn't smile once, until we reached the peak and the tomb came into view.

It had changed a lot over the centuries. Tourists had covered the walls of the cave with graffiti. And the ground was scorched from hundreds of teenage bonfires. Still, the site remained mostly intact. Propped up outside the cave, like a coin set on its edge, was the giant stone disc that the angels had moved to free Jesus Christ from his tomb. There were two indentations on the disc, like a large set of animal tracks, which were thought to be the handprints of the Archangel Gabriel himself.

"A lot of tourists like to stick their hands in the prints," I said to Fabiola. "If you want, you could do that, and I can paint your picture."

But she didn't seem to hear me. She had a dazed expression on her face, and her eyes were moist with tears. I followed as she tiptoed to the mouth of the cave and peered down the crumbling stone steps. Inside was the smooth slab of marble where Jesus's body had lain. You could still see the outline of his shroud.

"A lot of tourists like to lie on the outline of his shroud," I said.

But she ignored that suggestion as well. She fell to her knees, tears streaming down her face.

"Geez," I muttered. "I didn't realize you were so into Jesus."

She didn't respond. Her head was bowed. "I can't believe how much he suffered," she said. "It really reminds me how blessed we all are."

"Yeah, it's pretty cool." I cleared my throat. "So . . . wanna head out?"

She looked up at me with confusion. "Aren't we supposed to, like, say a prayer or something?"

"Well, I'm a monk," I said. "So I'm, like, always kind of praying."

"Don't you want to at least stay for a bit? And take it all in?"

"I'd love to," I told her. "But I've got things to do." I held up my hands. "These mitts aren't going to chop themselves off."

"Can't that wait a couple of hours?" she said. "I mean, this is the tomb of Jesus Christ. The holiest, humblest man to walk the earth."

"I know," I said. "Jesus is great, his tomb is great, everything about him is great, great, great."

She stood up and gaped at me. "Holy shit!" she said. "You're even competitive with *Jesus*?"

"How could I be competitive with Jesus?" I said, scoffing. "I'm a lowly monk! He's the king of kings! Besides, it's not even really, like, a fair playing field. I mean, he had all those connections."

"What are you talking about?"

"I'm just saying, like, if my dad was a famous god and my mom was a respected virgin and I was showered with frankincense, like, literally from birth, maybe I could start a religion too."

"You're so jealous."

"Okay, fine!" I said. "I'm jealous! Okay? I'm fucking jealous!"

I stared down at the ground. I could feel her eyes on my face, but I was too ashamed to look at her.

"Do you realize," I said, "that by my age Jesus had already performed six major miracles? I haven't even pulled off *one*."

"You're still young," she said. "There's time."

I shook my head. "I'll never catch up to him. It's mathematically impossible. I mean, even if I started performing miracles tomorrow and found some disciples right away, it would still be ten years minimum before the Romans arrested me. By the time they got around to crucifying me—if they even *decided* to do that—I'd be in my late thirties. And all of that's, like, best-case scenario. Like, if everything goes absolutely *perfectly*."

"You'll be kind of famous when they cut off your hands."

"Yeah, kind of," I murmured. "I mean, it's *something*. I'll have a niche, a brand. I'll be on the level of, like, a Hagaron."

"Who's Hagaron again?"

I sighed. "Exactly."

She laughed. "I'm sorry," she said, clearing her throat. "That was rude."

"No, I get it," I said. "You think I'm ridiculous."

"I just think you're being too hard on yourself. Maybe you should take a break from monk stuff and join our caravan. We're going to Carthage next."

"To see another tomb?"

"No, there's this music festival. Could be fun."

I nodded slowly, wondering what she meant by the invitation. My eyes had adjusted to the dark, and I could see her face clearly. The devil had worked hard to craft her features; every single inch was filled with beauty.

"Is that music festival the kind of thing where you need tickets?" I asked.

"Yeah," she said. "But, honestly, they're pretty easy to counterfeit. Admission is 'one shiny rock.'"

"Huh."

"Just think about it," she said.

The moon rose over the desert, lighting up the sky, revealing the entrance to heaven.

"It's getting late," I said.

"You're right," she said. "Let's go to bed."

We slept just a few feet apart—Fabiola in her cushioned tent and me just outside, on a pile of jagged stones I had collected. In the moonlight, through the fabric of her tent, I could see the outline of her chest, rising and falling with every breath. We were as alone as Adam and Eve in the Garden of Eden. Our only companion was an older, well-known gentleman. His name?

The Dark Lord Lucifer.

Since becoming a monk, I have managed to keep my vow of celibacy. In fact, in this regard I am even more accomplished than the average monk, since I was also celibate prior to taking my vows. While my schoolmates spent their youth in shameless pursuit of pleasure, flirting with girls, dating girls, and then marrying the girls and starting families with them, I spent my adolescence in monastic isolation.

That night, though, as the wind screamed like a banshee across the desert sky, the dark one came to tempt me. He whispered in my ear, filling my mind with thoughts of Fabiola. About the fairness of her hair and the sharpness of her mind and how she probably was the kind of person who gave really good hugs. Like, you know, how that's a thing, how some people, when they hug you, it just feels really, really nice.

I couldn't fall asleep. And as dawn began to break, I found myself hunched over my bed of jagged stones, examining their luster in the moonlight.

"Is this one shiny enough?" I asked.

"Oh yeah," she said. "That'll get you in for sure."

I grinned with excitement. "Really?"

"Dude, trust me. At these things, everyone is so f'd up on opium, they won't even check to see if it's a rock."

The sun was rising over the horizon, and the sky was lit with fire. I knew the devil had wormed his way into my soul. By leaving the desert, I was defying my vows and cursing God himself. But somehow I felt no shame. I imagined him gazing down at Fabiola, from atop his winged throne, and nodding with silent understanding.

"You sure you don't mind me tagging along?" I asked.

"Of course not!" she said. "We're gonna have a blast!"

My eyes filled with tears, and I embraced her. It was even

more spectacular than I had hoped. All at once, everything inside me eased, and I felt a sense of relief beyond anything I'd ever known. It was like eating a mouthful of grain after a yearlong fast. By the time I left her arms I was shaking.

"You okay?" she asked.

"Yeah!" I said, forcing a smile. "I'm good."

"Cool!" she said. "So...I guess we should get going. It's, like, a fortnight away, and we still have to pick up the rest of the group, so..."

I felt something tighten in my chest. "Who else is going?"

"Lots of cool people," she said. "My camp friends, this witch I know...my husband..."

I felt a soft ringing in my ears.

"Look," she said softly. "I'm sorry I didn't mention Marcus earlier. I obviously should have. I just assumed, because you were a monk, you weren't interested in me in that way."

I felt my face grow hot. "I don't know what you're talking about," I said. "I'm not interested in you in any way."

"I mean, you obviously are," she said. "When we hugged you started weeping. It was pretty nuts."

I said nothing.

"Why don't you come to the festival anyway?" she said. "That witch I mentioned, she's newly single. Maybe she'd be into you?"

"Out of the question," I said. "I'm sorry if this shocks you, but not everyone is as selfish as you."

She laughed incredulously. "Selfish? How am I selfish?"

"Geez, I don't know. You own twenty slaves, for example."

"They're not slaves," she said defensively. "They're my retinue."

"What's the difference?"

"There's a huge difference. They're, like, my colleagues."

"Cool, cool," I said. "So what are their names?"

Her soft cheeks reddened. "Excuse me?"

I leaned back and grinned, sensing my advantage. "If they're your colleagues, then surely you must know all their names."

She put her hands on her hips and cocked her head. "You want me to recite their names?"

"Sure, if you can."

"Fine!" she said. "The woman who dresses me is Penelope."

"Great," I said, clapping sarcastically. "That's one. Nineteen to go."

"You're such an asshole," she said.

I bowed my head. "If an asshole is one who unmasketh the truth, then verily I am an asshole."

"I can't believe I ever felt sorry for you," she said. "I thought you were a sad, pathetic loser. But you're worse than that. You're arrogant, you're cruel...You know what you are? You're the opposite of Jesus. You're the exact fucking opposite of Jesus."

She stared at me with rage, her nostrils flaring, her jaw clenched tight. It was painful to feel her hatred, but I didn't look away. I knew I was running out of time to see her face.

"Goodbye," she said. She started to walk down the mountain.

"Don't forget your fancy crates!" I shouted. "You wouldn't want to forget about your fancy, rich-girl crates!"

She didn't respond. It occurred to me, as she descended out of earshot, that it had not been a great last thing to say to her.

I stood on a rock and watched her until she disappeared below the tree line. I thought about the warmth of her embrace and how I would never experience anything like it again, and I started to feel a sensation in my chest that took me by surprise, because I didn't think it was possible, at this point in my life, to feel a new kind of pain.

I followed Fabiola's footprints down the mountain, but halfway down, I realized I'd gone off track. The steps had gone from small and dainty to large and oafish. I was nearing a stream when I heard a familiar groan.

It was Mordecai. He was lying by the water's edge, weeping into his hands. When I called his name, he roughly wiped his face and forced a neutral expression.

"Are you okay?" I asked.

"Of course," he said. "I'm great." He looked past me. "Where's the girl?"

"Gone forever."

He burst into tears, curled his limbs into a ball, and writhed around naked in the dirt. It occurred to me that I was not the only person suffering.

"I can't take it anymore!" he cried. "I need to unburden myself!" He took a few deep breaths and looked into my eyes. "This may shock you," he said, "but I kind of had a thing for Fabiola."

"Whoa!" I said, faking surprise the best I could. "Really? You mean that girl we just walked up the mountain with?"

He sobbed into his palms. "Yes!" he said, his voice muffled by his fingers. "The whole journey up, I was trying to impress her, and I just ended up making a fool out of myself!"

He turned away from me and wept. I could see his ribs pulsing through the thin skin of his back. He looked like a wounded animal. I sat down beside him and patted his cold, damp flesh.

"You're being too hard on yourself," I said. "You didn't do anything that embarrassing."

"What about when I drank your piss and ran into the woods?"

I flicked my wrist. "That was fine."

He looked up at me, his eyes as wide as a child's. "Really? It wasn't weird?"

"It was cool," I said. "It was badass."

He scrunched up his face, like someone preparing to receive a mighty blow. "Did she say anything about me?"

I knew, of course, that lying was a sin. But I decided to make an exception.

"She said you ruled," I said.

His eyes lit up. "Really?" he said. "Like, she used those exact words?"

"Yep," I said. "She told me, 'If he wasn't a monk, I'd be into him.'"

He collapsed onto the ground and let out a high-pitched laugh. "Yes!" he shouted. *"Yes!"*

A flock of birds in a nearby tree flew frantically into the sky. Their fear made sense: animals in our part of the desert were unused to cries of human joy.

"What else did she say about me?" he asked as I pulled him up to his feet.

"Let's head back to camp," I said. "I'll tell you all about it."

The five urns of "forgotten" grain were waiting for us at the bottom of the mountain, neatly stacked inside a wooden wheelbarrow. When Mordecai saw them, he shot me a pleading look. "Can I eat a few bites before you pee in it?"

"Don't worry," I told him. "I decided I'm going to stop doing that."

He embraced me.

By the time we got the grain back to camp, our fellow monks had grown too weak to move. Dominic was lying in the sand, staring up at the sky, too tired to shield his eyeballs from the sun. I grabbed a handful of oats and slowly fed them to him, making sure the flakes didn't get caught in his beard.

"Thank you," he said with relief. "You have saved me."

I smiled proudly.

"Okay," he said, rising slowly to his feet. "Now let's cut off those hands."

He grabbed a blade and lifted it high over his head.

"On three?" he suggested.

"Wait," I said. "This isn't a good time."

"Why not?"

I gestured at the other hungry monks. "I gotta feed them too."

I still intend to cut off both my hands. But right now, the truth is that I am unable to spare them. This week I'm using both to build tents for the elders. And next week, for Christmas, I'm going to surprise my fellow monks by sewing them some comfortable new clothes that cover up their entire penises, as opposed to just the holes. I have grain urns to mold and wells to dig. It seems like whenever I'm finishing a project, another one occurs to me. And sometimes, when I'm working, I think that maybe *this* is why God gave us hands. Maybe it wasn't to pleasure ourselves *or* to maim ourselves. Maybe our hands aren't for ourselves at all.

NEW CLIENT

Albie Katz, founder and CEO of Bright Stars Talent, was great at signing actors. Unfortunately, he was less great at providing them with actual careers. The "brightest star" he'd ever managed was a dancing chimpanzee named Mr. Mo, and he hadn't worked much since the formation of PETA. The humans Albie signed hadn't fared much better. One hardworking man eked out a living as an ass double. The best the rest could hope for was to play a murdered corpse on *CSI*. Albie knew he was a hack. And he would have quit years ago if it hadn't been for his wife, Rose.

Albie had proposed to her when they were still in high school, vowing to take care of her until the day she died. It was one of the few promises he'd kept, and he was determined not to break it. He couldn't afford full-time nursing care, but he still earned enough from his roster of corpses and asses to keep her well fed and content. She couldn't drink wine anymore, since it interfered with all her medicines, but he'd found a nonalcoholic brand at the Rite Aid, and every day he served her glass after glass on a silver-plated tray. She didn't talk much, but when he stooped down to kiss her, she closed her eyes and beamed, just like she had on their first date.

Albie had just tucked her in for her afternoon nap when he heard someone knocking on the door. It started as an eager tap but quickly intensified into a menacing thump. He didn't bother peeking through the peephole. He was eighty-one years old with stage-four emphysema. Who else could it be?

Death was taller than he expected, about eight foot six if you included his pointy hood.

"ARE YOU ALBIE KATZ?" he intoned in an unsettling baritone.

"Probably no use denying it," Albie said. "Come on in."

Death followed him into the bungalow, stooping to get under the doorframe.

"Can I get you a drink?" Albie asked.

"NO," Death said.

"You sure?" Albie grabbed a bottle of Rose's Rite Aid wine. "This is a great vintage—a grand cru from France. Happy to open it."

Death held up an hourglass. "SILENCE, MORTAL! YOUR TIME HAS COME!"

"Got it," Albie said. "Let me just say goodbye to Rose."

He stepped into the bedroom and looked down at his snoring wife. He was about to kiss her forehead when an idea occurred to him. It was a long shot, sure, but what did he have to lose? He reached into the closet and found his best blazer, the good-luck sharkskin he always wore to meetings. Then he cracked his neck and strolled back into the living room.

"Huh," he mumbled.

Death glared at Albie, his red eyes burning like a pair of embers.

"WHAT?"

"Oh, nothing," Albie said, flicking his wrist. "You probably wouldn't be interested."

"WHAT IS IT, MORTAL?" growled the reaper. "TELL ME."

"Well, I'm a talent scout," Albie said. "I represent actors—features and TV mostly."

He took out a business card and offered it up to Death. The reaper turned it over in his giant, bony hand.

"Anyway," Albie continued, "I guess I was just curious if you'd ever considered performing."

"HA-HA," Death said sarcastically.

"I'm serious," Albie said. "There's something about you. You've got a certain quality. A presence."

"THAT'S RIDICULOUS," Death said. "I'M NOT AN ACTOR."

"You've never even *thought* about it?"

"NO."

"Really?" Albie said. "I find that hard to believe. You're telling me you've never once performed in your entire life?"

Death was silent for a moment. His eyes were still burning but with slightly less intensity than before.

"I MEAN, I DID A LITTLE THEATER BACK IN HIGH SCHOOL," he said. "BUT THAT WAS A REALLY LONG TIME AGO."

"What kind of theater?"

"IT DOESN'T MATTER," Death said. "IT WAS A LONG TIME AGO. IT WAS STUPID."

"Come on," Albie begged. "I'm curious."

Death shrugged his knobby shoulders. "I GUESS THE ONE THING I DID THAT DIDN'T TOTALLY SUCK WAS THIS PRODUCTION OF *MACBETH*."

Albie raised his bushy eyebrows. "Whoa, you did *Shakespeare*? What part did you play?"

Death toed the carpet. "WELL, ACTUALLY," he said, "IF YOU MUST KNOW, I PLAYED THE PART OF MACBETH."

Albie whacked Death in the robe. "*Seriously*? The *lead*?"

Death waved his bony hands in the air. "IT'S NO BIG DEAL," he said. "IT'S MOSTLY JUST BECAUSE NO ONE ELSE WANTED TO DO IT."

Albie smirked. "*No one?*"

"WELL, I BEAT OUT A COUPLE OF GUYS," Death allowed. "BUT THEY WEREN'T VERY GOOD." His voice lowered. "I MEAN, ONE GUY WAS PRETTY GOOD, AND HE'D DONE A LOT OF PLAYS BEFORE, AND IT WAS MY FIRST TIME AUDITIONING, AND I GOT IT OVER HIM. SO, YOU KNOW, THAT WAS COOL." He shrugged again. "BUT LIKE I SAID, IT WAS A LONG TIME AGO."

"Sounds like you were pretty good."

"I MEAN, I WAS *ALL RIGHT*," Death said. "LIKE, AFTER THAT PLAY PEOPLE WERE DEFINITELY LIKE, 'YOU SHOULD PURSUE THAT.' LIKE, IF YOU LOOK AT

MY YEARBOOK, IT'S ALL 'SEE YOU ON BROADWAY!'—
STUFF LIKE THAT. BUT WHAT DID THEY KNOW? IT
WAS A LONG TIME AGO. IT WAS STUPID."

"Listen," Albie said. "There's this script making the
rounds right now, this Scorsese thing. He's looking for an actor who's over eight feet tall, with a baritone voice, eyes that
burn, not too experienced. I know you've got a full-time job,
but I'm sure he'd be grateful if you would at least go and
meet with him."

A smile flashed across Death's face, which he quickly sup-
pressed. "I MEAN, I GUESS IT MIGHT BE INTERESTING
TO MEET WITH HIM," he said. "JUST SO I COULD HAVE,
LIKE, A FUNNY STORY. YOU KNOW, AS A GOOF."

Albie nodded.

"I'M NOT EVEN SURE I'D EVEN WANT TO DO IT,"
Death stressed. "LIKE, EVEN IF HE WANTED TO CAST
ME IN A MOVIE, IT'S NOT LIKE IT'S MY BIG DREAM
TO BECOME SOME ACTOR."

"Of course not," Albie said.

"I MEAN, I DON'T MEAN ANY OFFENSE TO AC-
TORS," Death clarified. "IT JUST SEEMS LIKE A KIND OF
SILLY LIFE!"

"It's completely silly," Albie confirmed. "Always being
hounded by the press. People asking for autographs, trying
to be your buddy."

"YEAH!" Death said. "YEAH. STILL, IT MIGHT BE
FUN JUST TO MEET WITH SCORSESE. AS A GOOF,
YOU KNOW? JUST AS A FUN, STUPID GOOF."

"Right!" Albie said. "As a goof!" He gestured at the empty hourglass. "Of course, these meetings do take a little bit of time to set up."

Death hesitated. "I GUESS I DON'T HAVE TO TAKE YOU RIGHT THIS SECOND."

Albie grinned and whipped out a standard Bright Stars contract.

Death's hands twitched anxiously as he flipped through the official-looking pages.

"SHOULD I CHANGE MY NAME?" he asked. "IS 'DEATH' TOO JEWISH?"

"We can discuss later."

Death nodded and signed on the dotted line.

"OKAY!" he said. "SO WHAT NOW? IS IT, LIKE, A THING WHERE YOU CALL ME WHEN THERE'S SOMETHING?"

"Yes, I call you."

"COOL!" Death said. "COOL."

He started to leave but stopped in the entryway.

"ONE OTHER THING I MIGHT AS WELL TELL YOU ABOUT IS THAT I ALSO KIND OF PLAY A LITTLE MU-SIC. LIKE, MOSTLY GUITAR BUT ALSO PIANO AND BASS."

"Good to know," Albie said.

"AND I TOOK TWO YEARS OF TAP," Death said quickly. "OKAY! I'LL LET YOU GET TO WORK. YOU'LL CALL ME, RIGHT? THAT'S HOW IT WORKS?"

"I'll call you," Albie confirmed.

"OKAY!" Death said. "OKAY."

He floated out the door and vanished in a haze of wispy smoke.

Albie heard a rustling sound in the bedroom. He grabbed the Rite Aid wine, went inside, and kissed Rose softly on the cheek.

"Who were you talking to, sweetie?" she asked.

"I just landed a new client."

"Ooh, Albie," she said, beaming. "You're the best in the biz!"

He poured out two glasses, and they clinked them together.

"I'm not bad," he said.

THE GREAT JESTER

It is embarrassing to admit it, but the truth is, I've developed what the French might call *une reputation*. My barbs have bruised the breasts of many nobles. And some have grown to dread my jingly approach. But thus is a jester's lot! It is not my job to hold my tongue. Nay, it is my duty to ruffle royal feathers and summon Lady Wit upon this court!

Take last May Day, for instance. The king had thrown an elaborate feast for his good friend Lord Béarnaise. Béarnaise, as you know, is a powerful nobleman. But when he walked past me, I could not restrain my devilish impulses.

"Lord Béarnaise!" I said, waving my bell-clad arms to summon the attention of the court. "I am pleased to make your acquaintance! But I pray you refrain from being *saucy!*"

(The joke, in case you missed it, is that béarnaise is a type of sauce in addition to being Lord Béarnaise's name.)

Needless to say, Béarnaise was rather shocked by my impudence. He tried to walk away. But Lady Wit had seized me, and I could not help but speak her wicked words!

"I do believe that I have met your brother!" I said in my loudest tone. "Lord Hollandaise!"

(The joke there, in case you missed it, is that hollandaise is another type of sauce, in the manner of béarnaise.)

By this point the ladies were looking down at their laps, clearly overcome with merriment. As for the king, he was so amused that he closed his eyes and sighed.

"Okay, Havershire," he said, massaging the bridge of his nose. "Good one. You can stop now. Please. Stop."

One question I am often asked is: "How did you become the royal jester?" or "How is it possible that you're the royal jester?" I'm delighted that fans are interested in my artistic rise, and I have no qualms detailing it.

I was born in 1630 to the fifteenth Earl of Havershire. My father was not an entertainer but rather a skilled knight who fought beside the king when they were young. Some might presume that I owe my place in court to nepotism. And it's true that my father was close with the king and won him many territories and also saved his life on four occasions. But the jesting business is a meritocracy. In the coliseum of humor, only the wittiest men win the wit fights that happen in the wit-fighting area of the coliseum!

(What I mean by that, in case you missed it, is that you need to be really witty, and good at words, to be a jester, and it is not just who your father was, and so forth.)

I was by all accounts a precocious child. By the age of ten I was dancing original jigs at every meal. It was around this time that my father, undoubtedly seeing my potential, decided to send me to a year-round boarding school.

I struggled somewhat with my studies. But when it came to the subject of Wit, I was a grade A pupil. I spent each night practicing my barbs, shouting out rhymes and puns to my dorm mates. My routines were so beloved that my peers decided to elect me head boy. The prize was my own private room, on the far side of the school, away from the group.

Sadly, my parents never learned of this achievement. The influenza took them in 1647, and when I returned from my studies, it was to an empty house, the servants gone, the horses starved, the fields dry and ashen. The family fortune was exhausted, and I had no choice but to try to make a living.

Luckily by this point I was confident I had found my calling. I was already a jester in my soul. All I lacked was the official title.

The king was silent as I made my plea. England had not appointed a jester for ages. The last official clown was Old Man Chauncey, who had died in 1360. But his cottage was still standing, on the far side of the estate. And clearly I was his natural successor.

"So you would stay in that cottage?" the king asked at the end of my two-hour pitch. "At the far side of the estate?"

"Yes," I said.

"You mean the cottage on the other side of the moat, right? *Past* the hedge maze?"

"Yes."

"And you would stay over there full-time."

"Yes."

"So, just to confirm, you would be over there from now on. From now on, you would stay over there. Beyond the hedge maze. Away from my family."

"Yes."

I held my breath as the king deliberated.

"Okay, fine, whatever," he said. "You're the jester."

I was so overcome with joy that I began to dance, clapping and rhyming in ecstasy.

"You should go to the cottage now," said the king. "You should move there right now and just start living over there."

The rest, as the French might say, is *l'histoire*! (The history.)

The next twenty years were happy ones. Yes, it can be lonely to live by yourself in a small cottage without any family or friends. But I did have one regular visitor. Her name? Sweet Lady Wit!

By day, I drafted limericks. By night, I practiced jigs. And every Sunday I tended to my fool's cap, darning the purple fabric and buffing the golden bells until they shone.

I was engaged in this happy pursuit the night my world turned upside down. There was a knock on the door, and there he was.

The dwarf.

Before I continue with my tale, it is important to note that I am tolerant of dwarfs. Some view them with bigotry and prejudice. But I have always found the monsters friendly, and I don't see any reason for their capture. As far as I'm concerned, they should be free to live in peace, provided of course they refrain from magic.

That said, there is a difference between accepting dwarfs and inviting one into your home.

"Who are you?" I demanded.

"Name's Umphrey," he said.

Before I could respond, he shuffled past me and sat down on my bed. He was odd-looking even by dwarf standards, with a hard, distended belly and a red beard that hung down to his waist. He was completely naked except for a coarse brown rag, which he had loosely tied around his genitals.

"What are you doing here?" I asked.

"Rich man took me," he said. "Said I work for him now."

I smiled indulgently. He was a simple creature and clearly very lost. "I believe you want the stables," I said.

The dwarf picked at his beard, his bushy red eyebrows furrowed with confusion. "It was something other," he said.

"Whatever job the court has granted you," I assured him, "this is not where you belong. This is the jester's cottage."

The dwarf flashed a smile, revealing two rows of brownish teeth. "That's it!" he said with relief. "'Jester.' I'm the jester now."

That night, as the dwarf snored aggressively, I tried to process what had happened. There could not be two royal jesters. And therefore, Umphrey's appointment could mean only one thing. After twenty years of backbreaking service, of sacrificing everything to bring joy to the court, I had finally been awarded an apprentice.

I was proud to have been promoted to a position of management. But I was also somewhat anxious. Teaching the dwarf would not be easy.

I rose at dawn and paced around the hedge maze, plotting our curriculum. There was much to cover (puns, jigs). But if the dwarf applied himself, I saw no reason why he couldn't learn to jest within two decades.

I marched back to the cottage, eager to begin our first lesson. But when I opened my desk drawer, I was startled to find that it was empty.

"What happened to my limericks?" I asked the dwarf. "I had at least fifty in here!"

The dwarf averted his eyes. "Apologies," he said. "I thought it was ass paper."

"You thought it was *what?*"

"Ass paper," he said. "For wiping me ass."

"My God," I said.

"I am always doing this," the dwarf said with shame. "Thinking something be ass paper when it be some other kind of paper and then wiping me dirty ass with it."

"Couldn't you see that the pages were covered in words?"

"I never learned me letters," he said. "My mother, she be thinking me was cursed. So she sold me to the grave man for a farthing. I helped him dig his corpse holes, and he beat me something awful. It was a rough go." He hesitated. "There is something else to confess."

I eyed him nervously. "What is it?"

"I think I maybe broke yer indoor toilet. I took me shit in the hole, but it didn't go down any place."

"Umphrey," I said, "I don't have an indoor toilet."

I followed his gaze to my stove.

"Heyo," he said, hanging his head. "Heyo."

I shook my head in consternation. How on earth was I going to teach this poor creature about comedy?

Later that week, the dwarf was summoned to a royal banquet.

When I saw his invitation—a wax-sealed envelope doused with scent and stamped with gold—I was heartbroken. It's not that I was in any way envious of the dwarf. (I harbored no grudge for my own invitation's evident misplacement.) No, my upset was rooted in sympathy for my poor apprentice. It was criminal of the court to expect him to perform so early in his tutelage. He was so unsophisticated he could not even read his letter from the king.

"Havershire, please," he implored me. "Tell me the words."

I took the letter from him and patiently read it out loud. "'Dearest Umphrey, the crown requests your presence at a private ball. Please do not bring Havershire. He will say that he is invited, but he is not. Please come alone. Do not bring him. Come by yourself, and do not bring Havershire. Sincerely, the king.'"

The court's intentions were clear. They wished to subject the dwarf to a "private exam"—to see how he would fare without his tutor's expert supervision.

"Do not fear!" I told the dwarf. "A mentor never abandons his protégé!"

"Heyo," he said.

My plan was simple. While the dwarf entered through the castle gates, I would sneak in by cleverly shoving my body through the sewer hole. Once inside, it was an easy four-hour crawl up to the royal privy. If the dwarf ever needed my assistance, all he had to do was request to use the facilities, and there I'd be to offer him advice.

Unfortunately, my journey through the sewer took considerably longer than I anticipated due to several unexpected faintings. By the time I emerged from the toilet and rubbed myself off with a towel, the banquet was already in progress. I ran to the door of the privy and peeked through the keyhole to check on my pupil's progress.

I was horrified by what I saw. The dwarf had been placed directly beside the king—a cruel test to be sure. Needless to say, the poor creature was out of his depth. He did not understand even basic social etiquette. The waiters had served a course of walnuts and he had no idea which cutlery to use.

I watched as he whipped his head around, trying to get his bearings. Eventually, in desperation, he began to imitate the king, grabbing a cracker, wedging in a nut, and jerkily slapping it against the wooden table. It was around this time that I heard a peculiar noise: a loud, high-pitched cry. It was the princess. She was pointing at the dwarf and laughing.

Obviously, as a professional jester, I am no stranger

to the sound of laughter. I produce it at will, through my wit barbs. But there was something unusual about the princess's reaction to the dwarf. Typically, in my experience, when something amuses the royal family, they demonstrate their pleasure by flaring their nostrils, shaking their heads, or frowning with joy. The dwarf's imitation of the king, though, had elicited a different sort of laughter—a loud, unhinged spasm unlike anything I had ever heard.

The princess asked the dwarf to imitate more members of the court, and he obligingly went around the room, copying everyone's mannerisms. By the time he was finished, the entire court was laughing, including the king himself.

"Do another!" begged the princess.

The dwarf looked around the room. "I did you alls," he said.

There was a long silence and then the king's lips curled into a smile. "What about Havershire?" he said.

The dwarf glanced at the privy where I was in hiding. We locked eyes through the keyhole.

"I don't know how to do him," Umphrey said.

"Oh, come on," said Lord Béarnaise. "Havershire should be easy."

I was confused. Why would imitating me be easy?

The nobles began to chant. "Havershire! Havershire!"

The dwarf turned away from me and whispered to the group. He spoke so softly I could barely hear him.

"It is not nice," he said.

"Who cares?" said the king, throwing a piece of bread in his direction. "He's not here. Just fucking do him already!"

The dwarf nodded glumly. "Heyo."

The nobles cheered as the dwarf launched into his impersonation. I had trouble understanding it, because it so little resembled myself. First, he shrieked loudly and waved his hands like an imbecile. Next, he bowed deeply at the waist. Lastly, he turned around and mimed someone reacting to the performance—his face blank with misery and boredom. As the nobles started cheering, I finally grasped the meaning of the impression.

(The joke, in case you missed it, is that they do not consider me amusing. The joke is that they don't think I'm so good a jester.)

I know the nobles meant no harm by their laughter, but it was hard not to feel, as the French would say, a little *bleu* (a little blue). Another way to put it is that my heart was breaking.

I began to retreat back through the sewer hole. But then my sorrow gave way to resolve. I could still restore my reputation. All it would take was the performance of a lifetime.

I took a deep breath, kicked open the privy door, and threw both my arms up in the air.

"Hey nonny-nonny!" I cried. "Prepare to be jested!"

The king closed his eyes and covered his face with both his hands. "Oh my God," he said to no one in particular. "This is my nightmare. This, right now, is my nightmare."

I could tell I was off to a somewhat rocky start. I decided to jump straight into my "A material."

"It is time for a roast!" I shouted. "And I don't mean a dish of cooked meat! I mean a situation where I make jokes about those present. The term for both is 'roast.'"

The courtier hurried toward me, a stern look on his face. "Havershire," he said. "Can I talk to you in the hall?"

"I don't know!" I said, using my silliest voice. "*Can* you?"

"Please stop doing the voice," he said, his eyelids heavy. "Listen, I'm sorry, but it's over. You've been replaced."

My mouth went dry and my eyes filled with tears. Somehow, though, I managed to force a smile. "I did not know a courtier could jest!" I said.

"It's not a jest," he said. "And please stop doing the voice. Just speak in a normal voice."

I realized with shame that I was crying. That wouldn't do, of course. A jester's role is to entertain, not sadden. I took off my fool's cap and roughly wiped my eyes. I was about to put it back upon my head when the courtier gently pulled it from my hands.

"No," I begged him.

But it was too late. He had already walked back to the group and placed it upon the dwarf's scalp. I glanced at Umphrey. He was staring at the ground to avoid meeting my eyes.

"Please," I begged the courtier. "I know my jokes haven't always landed. We all have hits and misses. But I can be better! I can change my act!"

"Havershire—"

"I didn't know that you liked impressions!" I protested. "But I can do impressions too!" I crouched down a little. "Look, I'm Umphrey! I'm Umphrey!"

The crowd murmured softly.

"Yikes," said the princess. "So offensive."

The duke nodded. "Talk about punching down."

All at once, my sadness turned to rage. I had given my life to this court and did not deserve such rough treatment. If I were to leave, I decided, I would do so with a verse so barbed it would pierce the king straight to his heart!

"Attention, King!" I screamed.

The king took a swig of ale and reluctantly turned to face me. "What?"

"I will take leave of thy court!" I said. "But first hear mine wicked rhyme!"

I cleared my throat, determined to eviscerate him!

"Although my jests thou do like *not*. To me, your taste is foul as...as..."

To my embarrassment, I realized I was having some trouble coming up with a good rhyme for the word "not."

"It's okay," said the courtier, laying his hand upon my shoulder. "You don't have to finish it."

I shook him off. "Just give me a second!" I snapped. "Okay...I need to start again."

The crowd groaned.

"I'm starting again!" I said. "Okay. Here it goes. I'm starting again." I cleared my throat. "Although my jests thou do like *not,* to me your taste is foul as...as foul as..."

"How about 'snot'?" suggested the courtier. "Foul as snot?"

"Yes," I said, blinking away some tears. "That's where I was going. I would have gotten there."

I gave one final bow, then walked through the castle doors alone.

It wasn't easy getting used to life outside the court. I enquired around the village, to see if anyone was in need of jesting. But all I received were blank and baffled stares.

The only job I could find was digging ditches in the village graveyard. There was an opening, now that the dwarf was gone.

I moved into his old straw hut and took to drinking ale. A gallon would convince me that the court had made an error—that their poor taste in comedy was to blame for my dismissal. But every day at dawn, when the cock crowed me awake, my head would pound with the awful truth. It wasn't the court's fault. It was my own.

Years passed. My voice grew thin from underuse.

Sometimes at the tavern I'd overhear gossip from the court. How the dwarf had been awarded a piece of polished silver or had another ball thrown in his honor.

And then one day came the strangest rumor yet. The princess had given birth to a suspiciously small baby, with a bright mane of coarse red hair.

Several days later, I heard a soft knock on my hut.

I opened the door, and there he was.

The dwarf.

He'd been stripped of his finery and was naked except for a strip of sackcloth, which he'd tied over his genitals.

"Can I live here now?" he asked.

"Absolutely not," I told him. "You ruined my life, and I despise you."

The dwarf nodded. "I am always ruining things," he said. "Speaking of which, I think I have broke your outdoor toilet."

"I don't have an outdoor toilet."

I followed his eyes to my drinking well.

"Heyo," he said, hanging his head.

I tried to shut the door, but he blocked it with his stubby foot.

"Please," he said. "I have nowhere to go."

"There are rooms to let at the tavern."

"I have no money."

"Then make some."

"How?"

"I don't know! People seem to like you. Put on a show, sell tickets..."

"I don't know me letters," he reminded me. "Maybe you can help me do a show?"

I froze. For the first time in years, hopeful images flashed inside my head. Laughing fans, cheering crowds.

"Of course!" I whispered. "The two of us! Performing side by side, as a duo!"

The dwarf turned pale.

"I was thinking you would be more in the ticket-selling area," he said. "But if that is the price I must pay for your help, to be forced to perform by your side. If that is the 'devil's bargain' that I must make...the cross that I must bear...then I suppose I will endure that hell."

"Great!" I said. "I'll stand center stage, reciting verses. And after each line, maybe you can ring a bell or something?"

"I fear this show will fail," he said.

"Then you don't have to be a part of it!" I said stiffly. "Good day!"

The dwarf nodded sadly. "Heyo."

It wasn't until he turned to leave that I noticed the baby on his back, tied in place by a crude but careful knot. She was roughly the size of a potato, with curly red locks and large bright eyes. She babbled and laughed as her father trudged on, oblivious to their dire situation.

My thoughts turned to the royal hedge maze. In all my years at court, I had never been able to crack it. The course seemed unsolvable. But whenever I climbed up a hill and looked down at the labyrinth, I could easily see the proper route.

As I watched the dwarf shuffle through the graveyard with his baby, it occurred to me that I had lived my whole life as a man stuck in a maze, sprinting headlong down some futile trail. And now, for the first time ever, I was standing on a hill, watching myself from above, and all my years of struggle seemed so foolish, so absurd, that I couldn't help but laugh.

"I don't need to be in the show," I said.

Umphrey turned and beamed at me. "Are you sure?" he said. "If you want, you can come onstage for a minute at the start. And when people become angry, I can come up and save it?"

"That's okay," I said. "I'll just sell tickets."

He swallowed nervously. "I might be needing help with more than tickets."

"Like what?"

"I don't know," he said. "Building the stage. Making the signs. Selling the ale. Counting the moneys. Holding the moneys in a special place, so I don't think the moneys is ass paper and use it by mistake to wipe me dirty ass. I'm sure there is other things too, but those are the main things weighing on me."

"I can help with all of that," I said.

He threw his naked arms around my waist.

"There's no need for that," I said, blushing. "Anyone can plan a show."

He looked into my eyes. "Not anyone."

It is embarrassing to admit it, but the truth is, I've developed what the French might call *une reputation*. But such is a stage manager's lot! *The Great Jester Show* is a hit, and I am determined to keep it that way.

All day long I bustle around the theater, ensuring that everything is up to a high standard. First I scrutinize the stage, making sure the slats are level. Then I write and proof and print the evening's program. I make sure the props are set, the lamps are lit, and Umphrey's costumes are all fully mended. I uncork the ale cask, cue the musicians, and let in the general public. And then comes my favorite part. As the house fills up, I slip behind the curtain and gather silently with the cast and crew. Umphrey stands beside me, waiting for my signal. And when it's time, I whisper, "Places, people," and all of us go where we belong.

PHYSICIANS' LOUNGE, APRIL 1ST

-You wanted to see me, sir?

-Yes, Dr. Metzger. I'm afraid I've got some bad news.
I've been receiving complaints from your patients.
And I've decided I can't allow you to make April Fool's
jokes this year.

-Oh my God.

-I know you're disappointed, but my mind is made up.

-What about the one where I tell the patient I'm out
of anesthetic?

-No.

-What about the one where I put on a janitor's outfit,
grab a scalpel, and walk into the operating room just
as my patient loses consciousness? So he thinks he's
about to be operated on by a janitor?

-No.

-What about the one where the patient wakes up after his operation and I start shouting, "Where's my stethoscope? Where did I leave my stethoscope?" And then I stare at the patient's torso, with a look of horror, like I maybe left it inside his body?

-No.

-You can't do this to me! April Fool's Day is the highlight of my year. It's the only reason I finished medical school—to experience the holiday as a doctor.

-I'm sorry, Sam, but my hands are tied.

-What about the one where the patient wakes up and I'm wearing a robot costume, so he thinks he's been in a coma for eighty years. And I'm like, "Welcome to the future, Mr. Greenbaum. The world you remember is gone." You know, in a robot voice. So he thinks I'm a robot.

-I get it. The answer is still no.

-How could you be so cruel? I mean, for God's sake, what happened to the Hippocratic oath?

-"First do no harm"?

-That's what that meant?

-Yes.

-You sure it wasn't something about April Fool's?

-Yes.

-What about the one where I tell the patient his kidney operation was a grand success, but then, while I'm talking to him, I have an intern come in and say, "Dr. Metzger, you've got some dirt on your left shoulder." And I start to brush my *right* shoulder. And the intern's like, "No, your *left* shoulder." And I'm like, "This *is* my left shoulder." And he's like, "No, it's your right shoulder. What's the matter with you, Dr. Metzger? Don't you know your left from your right?" And then we both look at the patient's torso, with a look of horror, to imply, like . . .

-I know where you're going with this.

- . . . to imply, like, maybe I operated on the wrong kidney? Like, maybe I did the left one instead of the right one because I don't know the difference between my—

-No.

-At least let me workshop it!

-I'm sorry, Sam, but my decision is final.

-...

-April...Fool's.

-*No way!*

-I can't believe you bought that!

-*Man,* you got me good! Guess that's why you're the head of surgery.

-Pass me my robot mask. It's time to make the rounds.

RIDING SOLO: THE OATSY STORY

Growing up horse, I do not expect much from life. My ten older brothers all end up in stable. My sisters become glue.

When I am small, my father run off. That is not figure of speech. One day, for real, he just run into woods out of nowhere. Everyone is like: Whoa. That crazy.

It is not happy barn. But I have one escape: running. When I am doing gallop, I do not think about how little hay we have or where I will next find salt. I think only of wind in my mane as I surge through the air like bird. In that moment, I am happy. I am free.

Around this time I meet human. His name Paul.

Paul Revere.

He was not big star then. He was just regular guy from Boston—laid-back, funny, easy to carry. We become close and tell our secrets. Turns out we both have same dream: to make big mark on world. One night, when moon is up, we make pact: if one of us make it, we *both* make it. Together, there is no stopping us.

Then one day we see British coming, and I am like, This is it. This is our chance. We can ride to town and tell people British are coming, and it will be, like, this big thing. Paul is scared, and he is like, Are you sure that is good idea, Oatsy? And I am like, Trust me, I know what I talk about.

So Paul cannot run fast, because he has fat legs, and also, he is human. So he is like, Hey, can you do running part? And I am like, Of course. I will carry you whole way to town. And when we get there, you can do speaking part, since you are not horse and you know English and can talk. And he is like, Deal.

So then I carry him through brambles for hours, and he shouts, The British are coming, and next thing we know, everyone is cheering, and I neigh at Paul like, Told you so.

So army guy says, Okay, now you meet John Hancock and Sam Adams. And I am like, Whoa, this is big-time! But when we are walking to meetinghouse, something strange happens: Paul ties me to post. And I am like, Why not me go inside with you? And he is like, Well, you do not have tie and blazer, and also you are horse. And I am like, Huh. This weird.

And then person from newspaper jumps out, and he is like, Paul, Paul, how did you ride so long through night? And I snort, because of course Paul did not ride. *I* rode. He just clung to my back with eyes closed, crying whenever his face got brushed by leaf. So I smile at Paul, expecting him to correct newspaperman, but instead, he is like, "I rode so long because I care revolution." And I am like, Whoa. Paul change.

So after that, Paul become this big shot. Poem come out about him, and it is made into famous etching. And meanwhile, I unemployed. And my horse wife is like, How about you get work pulling carriage? And I am like, I saved country from British, I am not pulling around fatsos all day. And she is like, Have you been drinking? And I am like, I might have stopped by brewery and licked puddle, but what is wrong with that? I am full-grown horse. Back off! And she is like, What is wrong with you? And I say, There is nothing wrong with me; there is something wrong with world, because they do not realize it is me who made midnight ride! And she is like, Yeah, with Paul steering you. And that is when it happens. I kick her. And she is like, That's it, it's over, kids, let's go, pack up hay, we're leaving. And I am like, Wait. I sorry. Can we talk about this? But she is gone. She just run into woods out of nowhere. And I am like: Whoa. That crazy.

So then everything just fall apart. I go from licking brewery puddles to licking distillery puddles to just licking whatever puddles I can find, like, who cares, get it in me. And I find myself trotting around glue factory, thinking maybe I knock on door and tell them, Go ahead.

Everyone ask me, Why did Paul treat you so bad? I am not psychologist, but I have theories. For example, not everyone aware, but Paul has small penis. I could feel when he rode me. So maybe that make him crazy?

There is also romantic angle. Like, again, not everyone aware, but Paul's first wife, Mary, and I, we sort of had thing. One time, late at night, when no one was around, she was like, I would rather be with you, Oatsy, because I know midnight ride was your idea, and Paul stole credit, and also Paul has tiny penis, especially compared to horse, but I have to stay with Paul because of image. And I was like, Who cares about image? Let's just love each other and enjoy each other's bodies. And we did share one special night, but that is all I will say about it, because it is private.

I know that some people, when they read this book, they will think maybe I made some parts up. For example, some people will be like, How did you say those things to Paul? You are horse, you cannot speak, and you even said that yourself, early on in book, you said you cannot speak, but then there is so much speaking throughout entire book. Is inconsistent. Fine. They do not have to believe me. That is not why I write this; I write it for my thirty-seven horse kids, so they know the truth and not the lies.

Everyone says, You must be bitter. Paul Revere is big famous icon and your legs are failing and soon you will be glue, probably within a few hours, because you are in cage at the glue factory and they are doing you, like, pretty soon. But anger is like salt lick. Every day it shrink and shrink. And I think that when I die, my last thought will not be Paul's betrayal; it will be that moonlit night, that ride through the brambles, the feeling of wind in my mane as I surged through the air like bird. For a moment, I was happy. I was free.

MENLO PARK, 1891

—Still from Newark Athlete, *Edison Studios, 1891*

"Sorry to bother," Jed murmured, "but I think I maybe made another mix-up."

Thomas Edison squinted at the boy. He'd known for some time that Jed was unintelligent. But lately he'd begun to suspect that the boy was an actual medical idiot.

"What is it now?" Edison muttered.

"Did you say to mix in five centiliters?"

"No," Edison said. "Five *milliliters*."

A nearby beaker exploded, showering them both with shards of glass.

"Sorry," Jed said.

Edison closed his eyes and rubbed his throbbing temples. He'd hired the local high school boy to help with basic lab work. But even the simplest of tasks were beyond his capabilities. The boy's best hope of contributing to science was to let doctors dissect his head, so they could study the brain of a moron. There was simply no other use for him.

Except, perhaps, for one.

"What do I do?" Jed asked.

"Just stand here," Edison said. "In this spot."

He roughly positioned the boy in front of his new apparatus, a square contraption built of tin and glass.

"Okay," he said. "Action!"

"What?" said the boy.

"Do some action," Edison said. "With your body."

"What kind?"

"It doesn't matter," Edison said impatiently. "Here." He handed the boy a pair of oblong wooden clubs. "Swing these around."

Jed took the clubs and flailed them around over his head. It was upsetting to watch, but of course it didn't matter what Jed did. The point was to showcase his glorious new invention: the kinetograph. Thanks to its novel high-speed shutter system, the device could produce a living photograph—what Edison liked to call a "motion picture." The phonograph had brought him fame. The light bulb had brought him riches. But this machine would bring him immortality. This machine, he knew, would change the world forever.

Edison entitled his film, somewhat sarcastically, *Newark Athlete*. He knew the reception would be positive, but when he screened it in his lab, the response surpassed his wildest expectations. Hundreds of reporters were crammed into the space, and when the film was over, they stood up and cheered, laughing and hollering like children.

Edison rarely smoked, but the occasion seemed to call for a cigar. He snapped at Jed, and the boy ran over to bring him one.

"Any questions?" Edison asked the crowd.

Before he could call on anyone, the reporters began to shout, as if alarmed.

"What is it?" Edison asked, looking around in confusion.

"It's him!" cried a reporter, pointing his finger at the boy. "The Newark athlete!"

Edison turned to Jed, who was smiling stupidly, surprised by the attention.

"Ah yes," chuckled Edison. "That's the boy I used to display my invention. Anyway...questions?"

A reporter raised his hand. "Is it okay if I ask the *boy* a question?"

Edison was baffled. Jed had not had any involvement whatsoever in the invention of kinetography. But he saw no harm in obliging the reporter.

"I suppose that's fine," he said.

The reporter turned to Jed and blushed. He looked a bit nervous. "Wow," he said. "This is exciting. First of all, I just want to say, I love your movie."

Edison choked a little on his cigar. It wasn't Jed's movie— it was his. He watched with mounting annoyance as the reporter continued to ramble.

"I think something we'd all like to know is: what kind of preparation did you have to do for your role?"

The boy shrugged. "Not much," he said. "I kind of just stood in front of the lens."

The reporter nodded. "So you just, like, channeled it. You

were like, 'I'm going to *be* this Newark athlete' and then you *were*."

The boy shrugged. "I guess."

"Wow," the reporter said, shaking his head with awe. "Holy shit."

Edison smiled curtly. "Okay," he said. "That was fun. To interview the boy. Any questions for me? The inventor of kinetography?"

"Jed!" shouted a reporter in the back. "Do you have any advice for people starting out who want to be in pictures?"

Jed shrugged. "I don't know."

"Please!" the reporter begged.

Jed scratched his head. "I guess...follow your dreams?"

The crowd applauded.

Edison tried to regain their attention, but it was too late. The reporters had rushed past him and were surrounding the boy, peppering him with questions about his personal life.

"No, I'm not seeing anyone right now," he heard Jed say.

"Not seeing anyone, like, *at all*?" asked a reporter. "Or, like, not *seriously dating* anyone?"

Jed shrugged. "I guess, like, 'not seriously dating.'"

"So you, like, hook up and stuff."

Jed nodded. "I hook up."

Edison realized with amazement that somehow he had been pushed out of his own laboratory. Reporters wrestled past him, brandishing cameras and blasting flash powder in his face. Edison coughed as his throat filled up with phosphorus. And as he sunk to his knees, it occurred to him that his prediction had come true: this time, he'd changed the world forever.

TOM HANKS STORIES

"I saw Tom Hanks at a drugstore in West Hollywood. He didn't try to cut the line or anything. He just got in the back and waited, like he was a regular person. I couldn't believe he was buying his own toothpaste! I figured a movie star like him would have someone to do that for him. But not Tom Hanks. He's just a down-to-earth, classy kind of guy."

"I drove Tom Hanks to the airport once. He was normal the whole ride. Didn't scream at me or threaten my life. Craziest thing: he stayed in a seated position the entire time. No levitating."

"So I'm waiting outside the Paramount lot, hoping to see a celebrity, and out comes Tom Hanks. Just walking, using his legs. So I say, 'Would you please sign my tee shirt?' Then I brace myself: you know, expecting him to vomit bile on me, out of pure disgust. But instead, he says, 'Sure,' and *signs my shirt*! Here's the craziest part: he used a *pen*. I figured he'd probably plunge a syringe into my chest and sign his name using blood from my heart. You know, to make a point about my comparative worthlessness and the expendability of my life relative to his. But, no. He uses a regular pen. Like the kind you would find in a store. If there's a classier guy on earth, I'd like to meet him."

"I'm sitting on a bench with my family when Tom Hanks walks by on the sidewalk. I don't know what to say, so I just shout out, 'Hey, Tom!' And he stops. So I figure okay, this is it. I'm going to die. He's going to take out a gun and shoot me point-blank in the face, which, let's be honest, is what I deserve. I mean, the guy has a million important things to do, he's a huge celebrity, and here I am, stopping his walking. At the very least, I figure he'll make love to my wife or my daughter in front of me. You know, to prove a point about how the world is his and he can take what he wants and I'm just like an insect to him. But none of this transpires. Instead, he just smiles at me and says, 'Hey.' Class act all the way."

"I once saw Tom Hanks from across a crowded parking lot. Get this: the guy was wearing pants. Like, regular, human pants. With a button and a zipper and the whole deal. You don't have to believe me. But I swear to Hanks I'm telling you the truth."

ADOLF HITLER: THE *GQ* PROFILE

Adolf Hitler has a question about the fries.

The waiter is clearly stunned. We're at Fork and Twig, one of the most exclusive eateries in Beverly Hills. Customers don't typically ask questions. But, as our server will soon learn, there is nothing typical about Adolf Hitler.

"Can I get the fries without all that truffle shit?" he asks.

"You mean the aioli?"

"Whatever the fuck it's called."

The waiter can't help but smile at Hitler's brashness. He dutifully marks the request down on his notepad and hurries off to tell the kitchen. Hitler leans across the table and flashes me a conspiratorial grin.

"Sometimes," he says, "you just want what you want."

Adolf Hitler has made a career out of wanting what he wants. I could go through the superlatives, not like anybody needs me to: one war, two fronts, six million Jews, all before the age of sixty. Even by celebrity standards, the numbers are impressive.

"Hitler exists in his own category," says *Smithsonian* magazine editor Chris Davenport. "I mean, you've got your Pol

Pots and your Stalins. They're major brands. But let's be real. When you've got to move units off the newsstand, there's only one face you're sticking on the cover."

Given his global celebrity, you would expect Hitler's presence to attract more attention at Fork and Twig. But despite the occasional stare, we seem to be flying below the radar. It's obvious why: Hitler is not a typical celebrity. There's no handler, no agent, no sycophantic entourage. There's just, well, Hitler.

"It's easy to forget where you came from," he says. "Especially in this town."

The fries arrive—plain, of course—and Hitler shoves a wad of them into his mouth.

"These aren't going to be enough," he tells the waiter. "Bring us another order."

The waiter runs back to the kitchen, and Hitler flashes me a wink.

"It's the Austrian in me," he says. "I can't resist free food."

Another thing he can't resist these days is Brazilian jujitsu. He was thirty minutes late to our encounter because a sparring match went long.

"This guy tried to arm bar me," he says, smirking. "Let's just say it didn't go exactly as he planned."

It's a classic Hitler statement. Humble, witty, understated—but burning with competitive fire.

Yes, Hitler's style has mellowed since his heyday in the forties. Gone are the Hugo Boss power suits of old, replaced by a muted ensemble from Rag & Bone. But don't let the understated cardigan fool you. Hitler's ambition glows as bright as ever.

"Everyone knows he's working on something," says UN spokesman Carol Torres. "No one knows exactly what it is. His people won't reveal much to us. But rumor is, it's his most ambitious genocide in years."

When I ask him for specifics, he's evasive. "You're gonna get me in trouble," he says. He picks up my tape recorder and talks directly into the microphone. "No comment!" He laughs, and I can't help but join in. This isn't his first rodeo.

You would think someone as accomplished as Hitler would be content to rest on his laurels and cede the limelight to the next generation of homicidal dictators.

But that would be typical.

"I don't sleep much," Hitler admits when I ask him about his legendary work schedule. "I know my hours are nuts. Anyone who saw me work would say, 'That's unsustainable.' But look, when you love the work? When the work means something to you? You don't want to waste a day." He smiles ruefully. "Of course, sometimes there are casualties."

I don't press him for details, but it's obvious to what he's referring. Hitler recently ended a long-term relationship with iconic supermodel Öo. The breakup, by all accounts, was amicable. But a source close to the pair told me that Hitler's obsession with his work is what ultimately tore them apart.

"It's hard to be a good boyfriend when you're in Brazil forty weeks a year, planning a major genocide."

Hitler grabs the last fry, a crisp, burnt nubbin, and tosses it into his mouth.

"Where's our second order?" he asks. "It never came."

A younger Hitler might have reacted with anger. But the man sitting across from me just throws up his hands in frustration. It's a gesture that speaks volumes. There are some things in life you can't control—no matter who you are.

A funny thing happened to Hitler when he lost his iPhone. He realized that he didn't really miss it.

"I was helping with some project in Iraq," he says with characteristic modesty. "And the rain started pouring from the sky. And everyone started running. And I thought, *There's nowhere else I'd rather be than right here. Right now.*"

In the six months since this epiphany, Hitler's been operating in a different gear.

The Brazilian jujitsu is just part of the puzzle. He begins each morning with a wellness routine designed to "counteract the bullshit." It all starts with a long solo hike into the hills, followed by an hour of sun salutations.

When I point out that yoga isn't exactly "on brand," Hitler nods good-naturedly. "Don't tell CAA," he says. "They'll drop me like a bag of shit."

He's in the middle of a hearty laugh when the moment is interrupted. A teenage fan has walked up to our table.

"I'm sorry to bother you," he says. "Is there any way I can get a selfie?"

"Make it quick," Hitler says.

He gamely poses while the teenager bursts into action, snapping the shot with the precision of a seasoned paparazzo. Hitler winces at the flash and shakes his head wearily as the teenager heads for the door without even so much as a thank-you.

I try to steer the conversation back to Hitler's exercise routine, but it's clear that a pall has been cast over our meal.

I ask the obvious question. Doesn't Hitler like having fans?

"It's nice when people appreciate the work," he says diplomatically. "But this..." He gestures at the fan, then my tape recorder. "This is not the work. This is...something else."

Hitler goes to take a call from his publicist, and I realize, with shame, that Hitler is absolutely right. What is the point of this interview? What is the point of our entire bankrupt culture?

I force myself to look outside the window. Flashy cars whiz down Rodeo like shiny neon bullets. Teenagers pose with selfie sticks, sucking in their cheeks like models in some nightmare acid freak show. The air is thick with man-made smog. You don't need to ask Siri to find out what's happened; the times have changed.

I feel myself begin to cry: for our future, for the world, and for myself.

It's around this time that Hitler returns to the table. He looks into my eyes, and I brace myself for some harsh words.

And that's when he does it.

He smiles.

You've seen it on book covers, in newsreels, and in propaganda films for over fifty years—that playful grin, a mix of earnest boyishness and charm. But until you've seen it up close—until you've *beheld* it—it's hard to explain just what it means.

It means: We're here. Right now. In this moment.

And maybe this moment is about more than how many Instagram followers we have. Maybe our emotions aren't reducible to algorithms. And maybe, just maybe, life is a little bigger than that phone that keeps vibrating in our pocket.

Adolf Hitler has gone through so much: ups and downs, highs and lows. And now, sitting here across from him, I think I finally know the reason why: he did it for us. We can't all be Hitler. But maybe, if we try, we can glimpse some of the wisdom he's learned. Hitler has committed genocide against his insecurities. He's cremated his doubts and gassed his fears. He's been down, but he's not out. Hell, in some ways he's just getting started.

Hitler lets out a whoop as the waiter comes back to our table.

He's brought more fries.

ANY PERSON, LIVING OR DEAD

If you could have dinner with any person, living or dead, whom would you choose? Aristotle? Catherine the Great? Mahatma Gandhi?

Luckily for you, recent advances in time travel technology have made it possible to turn this age-old fantasy into reality.

FREQUENTLY ASKED QUESTIONS

How does it work?

As soon as your payment clears, our skilled technicians will travel back in time to capture, sedate, and abduct a historical figure of your choosing.

Is sedation necessary?

Unfortunately, yes. Most historical figures are confused by the concept of time travel. When we appear in their homes, they often flee or become physically combative. Once sedated, though, guests usually accept their "invitation" to dinner.

What should I talk about with my guest at our dinner?

Unfortunately, conversation at your dinner will probably be minimal. Most historical figures do not understand modern English. Also, it is unlikely that your guest will be in the mood to talk. Time travel is extremely physically traumatic. Each trip involves more than six and a half minutes of free fall, 900 g's of spinal pressure, and temperature swings ranging from 150 degrees Fahrenheit to 30 degrees below freezing. By the time guests arrive at dinner they are almost always unconscious.

Are any historical figures "off-limits"?

We regret to inform you that William Shakespeare is no longer available for dinners.

In the first few years of our operation, Shakespeare was one of our most sought-after guests, appearing at dinners at a rate of three to five times a week. These appearances put a heavy strain on him, both mentally and physically. He began to recognize our technicians, and whenever he spotted them, he would burst into tears and run screaming through the streets of London. Many of our technicians are former Navy SEALs, and they seldom had difficulty capturing the unathletic Shakespeare. But the amount of violence needed to subdue the famous playwright grew to unacceptable levels. After a series of tribunals, the United Nations concluded that we can no longer "invite" William Shakespeare to events.

Can I read any testimonials?

Absolutely. The following reviews come from actual, satisfied customers.

Bob from San Antonio:

"I wanted to meet Da Vinci because I saw that movie about his code and I wanted to know if it was real. The first thing he said was *'Oh mio Dio,'* which a technician told me means *'Oh my God.'* Then he started whispering *'diablos.'* I guess he thought he'd died and was in hell? Anyway, I tried to ask him about his code, but he was pretty strung out from his trip and all the sedation, so I just let it go. It was cool to see his clothes; he had a brown shirt with funny wooden buttons."

Mike from Fort Wayne:

"It was pretty wild hanging out with John Lennon. The first thing he said when he came through the portal was 'I need my stomach pumped.' I think he thought he was having a drug experience.

"He was really fidgety, so a technician decided to put him in a restraint chair. When Lennon saw the straps, he freaked out. The scientists kept warning him to 'be good,' but Lennon wouldn't stop flailing, so one of the technicians had to slap him. When the restraints were finally on, Lennon's body went limp and he started to cry.

"I was a little nervous to talk to him, because he's such a big celebrity, but eventually I worked up the nerve. It was during dessert, after Lennon had been quiet for about an hour. Two technicians propped Lennon's head up, and I said to him, 'Mr. Lennon, I just want to tell you that I love your music and I cried for hours the day you got assassinated.' As soon as I said it, I realized I'd made a bad mistake. Mr. Lennon's eyes got wild, and he started saying, 'Who's gonna kill me? When's it going to happen? You've gotta tell me! This is my life! *My life!*' He got so angry that he managed to rip off one of his restraints, which is incredible because they're made of steel. With his free hand he reached for a butter knife, and the technicians had no choice but to shoot him with a tranquilizer dart. It hit him right in the center of his chest. He looked down at the dart for a few seconds in total shock. Then he looked up at me and started to weep, with a look on his face like *How could you have done this to me? What have I done to deserve this?* I could tell he wasn't thrilled about the whole situation, but at the end of the day, it's like *Hey, buddy, you're a celebrity. This is what you signed up for.*"

UPWARD MOBILITY

As Dylan boarded his boss's private jet, he reflected on how blessed he was. A year ago, he'd moved from Omaha to Hollywood without any prospects whatsoever. His small Christian college hadn't offered any film courses, and his only work experience had been at the local air conditioner factory. Somehow, though, against all odds, he'd landed a job with Jack Krieger, the most powerful studio boss in town.

It wasn't easy being Jack's personal assistant. Each day, it fell on Dylan to organize Jack's schedule, answer his phone calls, make his reservations, pick up his dry cleaning, polish his shoes, write memos to his employees, write letters to his shareholders, write birthday cards to his children, bring him cocaine, remind him what day it was, and handle any other task his boss considered "bullshit." Dylan's salary was pitiful and his workload gigantic. But the job offered great upward mobility. On his first day of work, Jack swore to Dylan that the harder he toiled, the more he would learn and the brighter his future would be. And it was this happy promise that kept Dylan motivated, all the way up until the moment Jack's private jet exploded and he died.

• • •

Dylan squinted through the hazy, chest-high clouds. He could see his boss ahead of him, looking around with annoyance.

"Dylan?" he called out. "Where the hell are you?"

Dylan hurried over as quickly as he could. At the time of the jet crash, he'd been sitting illegally in the aisle so his boss could use his chair as a footrest. As a result of this positioning, his death had been far more gruesome than his boss's. There was a long, jagged gash extending from his forehead to his neck and a spiky piece of fuselage protruding from his chest. He was also missing his left leg. Jack had some light char marks on his suit but otherwise looked fine.

"Where the fuck are we?" he demanded.

Dylan's shoulders tensed. It was his responsibility to keep track of every aspect of Jack's life, from his Wi-Fi password to his Social Security number. The more confused Jack was, the worse Dylan was doing at his job.

"Don't worry," Dylan promised. "I'll find out what's going on."

He hopped through the clouds, struggling for balance on his one remaining leg. Within moments, he was back at Jack's side, flipping through an informational pamphlet.

"Okay," he said, a little out of breath. "Basically, the situation is that we died in a plane crash and now we have to wait in line to see Saint Peter."

"Do I have to go up there myself?" Jack asked. "Or can you just do it for me, like with the DMV?"

"I think you have to go up there yourself."

"This is bullshit!" Jack said. "Is there at least some kind of express line? Like a business class type of deal?"

Dylan scanned the pamphlet. "I'm sorry, sir," he said. "I think there's just one line for everybody."

"Fuck!" Jack said.

He eyed the people standing in front of them in line, a large Midwestern family who had apparently died in some kind of horrible roller-coaster crash.

"Christ," he said. "Can you believe how fat this country's getting?"

Dylan gave a practiced nod. Several times a week Jack would go on a hateful tirade against fat people, and part of Dylan's job was to normalize his boss's viewpoint on the subject.

"They should all be castrated," Jack said. "They should make a law that if you weigh a certain amount, it's illegal to have children."

"Absolutely," Dylan said. "Good idea, sir."

"You know we had to make the damn seats bigger?" Jack said. "All over Wisconsin and Michigan, we had to rip out thirty rows in every movie theater so the fatsos could fit their bodies into the goddamn seats. And we had to double the size of the drink holder. Can you imagine? We had to *double* it!"

"I'm sorry," Dylan said.

"If these people get any goddamn fatter, pretty soon every theater's gonna be just one big seat, and it'll also be a toilet, so the fatso doesn't ever have to get up. He can just sit there watching *Ironman* while shitting out his nachos like an animal. Have you ever seen one of them eat nachos? They don't stop to breathe! It's nacho, nacho, nacho, nacho—"

Dylan politely cleared his throat.

"What?" Jack snapped. He wasn't used to being interrupted.

Dylan gestured subtly with his head.

"Oh," Jack said. "Right."

They had come to the front of the line. Saint Peter was glaring down at them from his lectern. Dylan couldn't help but notice that he happened to be overweight.

"Welcome to your judgment," said the saint.

"How long's this gonna take?" Jack asked.

"Excuse me?"

Dylan forced a laugh. "Sorry!" he said to the saint. "He's just been through some trauma."

He quickly hopped forward so that he was standing in between his boss and Saint Peter. Despite the circumstances, his confidence was high. If there's one thing he'd mastered in his three years as Jack's assistant, it was getting Jack into exclusive establishments. Just last week he'd gotten him a table at Trois Mec, without a reservation. How hard could heaven be?

"I'm Mr. Krieger's assistant," he explained. "I think you'll find that my boss more than qualifies for heaven."

"I don't see how," said the saint as he flipped through Jack's file. "I mean, his Good Deeds page is blank. I've never seen that before, not even with babies."

"Holy shit," Jack murmured to his assistant. "This fatso's got it in for me. What are we going to do?"

"Don't worry," Dylan whispered reassuringly. "I've got an idea." He smiled at Saint Peter. "Sir, if it's not too much trouble, I'd love for you to look into my boss's Charitable Contributions."

Saint Peter begrudgingly flipped to the back of Jack's file. His eyes widened with shock.

"As you can see," Dylan said, "Mr. Krieger recently gave more than one million dollars to charity. That makes him one of the most generous people on the planet."

It was technically true. Dylan remembered the day Jack had made the donation. He'd just found out that he owed five million dollars in back taxes. "Get me my Jews!" he'd screamed. Within minutes, Dylan had called up Jack's accountants, and together they had figured out a way for Jack to dodge most of the taxes by making a series of "strategically timed charitable donations."

"I suppose it's something," muttered Saint Peter. He was clearly upset by the loophole Dylan had found.

"Can I go in now?" Jack asked.

"No," said Saint Peter. "Good Deeds are just one category. We also take into account your Life's Work."

Dylan felt his stomach rumble. This wouldn't be easy.

"According to your file," Saint Peter said to Jack, "you've released over a hundred films into the world." He put on his spectacles and squinted at the list. "Why do so many have the same name?"

"Those are sequels," Jack explained.

"What's *Bad Doctor*?"

"That was a starring vehicle for Zac Efron," Jack said. "It's about a stoner who cheats his way into medical school so he can get access to the drugs. And he bangs all the hot nurses."

"What about *Bad Cops*?"

"Dave Franco and Zac Efron. They cheat their way into a police academy so they can get access to the drugs. Then they bang all the hot evidence girls."

"What are 'evidence girls'?"

"It's something we had to make up," Jack admitted. "You know, so they had girls to bang."

"These movies sound like filth," said Saint Peter.

Dylan cleared his throat.

"What about *The Rising of Our Lord*?" he said.

Saint Peter folded his arms. "Excuse me?"

"It's one of Mr. Krieger's films," Dylan explained. He leaned across the lectern, flipped through Jack's file, and pointed out the title.

"There!" he said. "In 2004. A dramatic portrayal of Jesus Christ's heroic Crucifixion."

Again, Dylan's point was technically true. Jack had a very vocal policy of green-lighting one "Jesus movie" a year so the studio could "buttfuck the Christians out of all their money." *Rising* alone had grossed more than 300 million dollars.

"It's a very moral movie," Dylan told the saint. "A gripping tribute to our Lord. Have you seen it?"

"No," the saint said coldly.

"Well, would you mind asking around among your colleagues?" Dylan inquired. "I bet some of them are familiar with it."

Saint Peter's eye twitched. "Very well."

He slipped through the gate and returned moments later. His jaw was tightly clenched, and the blood seemed to have drained from his face.

"Something wrong?" Jack asked.

Saint Peter took a long, slow breath. When he finally spoke, his voice was soft and clipped. "If it's not too much trouble," he said, "God would like you to sign his DVD."

Dylan smiled proudly and handed his boss a pen.

"Anything else?" Jack asked as he scribbled down his autograph.

"No," Saint Peter muttered. "God has recommended that you receive entrance to heaven."

"Booyah!" Jack said. "Wait, wait, hold on, though." He leaned across the lectern. "There's cocaine in there, right?"

Saint Peter nodded sadly. "There's cocaine."

Jack pumped his fist.

"The system is broken," Saint Peter mumbled to himself. "The system does not work."

Dylan felt guilty for demoralizing Saint Peter, but he couldn't help but feel a surge of pride. He'd managed to help his boss through a major, unprecedented crisis. It was his greatest feat as an assistant yet. Who knew what it would lead to?

His mood deflated, though, at the sight of something happening in the distance. A pair of rosy-cheeked cherubs were hanging a sign on the gates.

HEAVEN CLOSED FOR 100,000 YEARS.

"What's that mean?" Dylan asked nervously.

"Just what it says," said the saint. "We can't let anyone in for the next one hundred millennia."

Dylan's mouth went dry. "Why not?"

"Unfortunately, heaven is very, very small. We only have room to let in a very select, privileged few."

"Like business class!" Jack pointed out.

"Yes," the saint said bitterly. "Like business class." He turned to Dylan and bowed his head with genuine remorse. "I'm sorry we didn't get to you. You seemed like a good person."

"So what happens to me?" Dylan asked in a small, frightened voice. "Where do I go?"

Saint Peter shrugged. "I don't know."

"You don't *know*?"

"I mean, I have some idea."

"Is it hell?" Dylan asked. "Am I going to hell?"

Saint Peter threw up his hands with frustration. "What do you want me to say?"

"I want you to tell me the truth."

"Then, yeah," Saint Peter said. "You're going to hell."

"Like, *full* hell?"

"Yes," said the saint. "Full hell. With the fire and the screaming. The whole thing."

Dylan's eyes filled with tears. "Oh no," he said. "No."

Jack laughed. "Oh man," he said. "Sucks to be you!" He turned back to Saint Peter. "So...what's next for me? I assume I gotta sign some bullshit or whatever?"

Saint Peter nodded dutifully. "Yes," he said. "Right here, in the back of God's book. Just fill out your name..."

Jack wrote down his name.

"And your birthday..."

Jack wrote down his birthday.

"And your Social Security number."

Jack looked over his shoulder at his weeping assistant.

"Hey, what's my Social?"

Dylan instinctively started to recite it. But a few digits in, his mind began to turn. He thought of the Christmas he'd spent on the phone to Time Warner, arguing a three-dollar charge on Jack's behalf. He thought of the thousands of emails he had printed out on his home computer because Jack didn't like to "read shit on a screen." He thought of how he'd spent his final moments on the planet, contorting his body to create more space for his boss's feet. When he spoke, his voice had an uncharacteristic edge to it.

"What happens if he doesn't know his Social Security number?"

A smile slowly spread across Saint Peter's face. There was a conspiratorial gleam in his eye. "If he can't prove his identity," he said, "I can't let him into heaven."

"Whoa, whoa, whoa," Jack said. "This is ridiculous. What are you saying, that I'm an imposter or something?"

"I'm sorry, sir," said the saint. "I'm just having trouble believing you are who you say you are. I mean, surely the real Jack Krieger would know his Social Security number." He turned to Dylan with a goading grin. "Surely the *real Jack Krieger* would know the basic facts of his own life."

Dylan realized, with shock, that his fear of his boss had vanished. In its place was something close to glee.

"Young man," Saint Peter said, "I don't think we've been officially introduced." He stretched out his palm and nodded at him. "What's your name?"

Dylan grinned at his boss as he shook Saint Peter's hand.

"I'm Jack Krieger," he said.

Jack's face turned pale. "This is bullshit," he said in a strangled whisper. "He's lying!"

"Don't worry," said Saint Peter. "I'll confirm his identity."

He handed Dylan a pen.

"Write down your Social, your Wi-Fi password, and your children's birthdays."

Dylan neatly printed out the information.

"Well, that settles it," said Saint Peter.

Dylan laughed with delight as a pair of cherubs scooped him up on a throne of gold and rubies. His injuries magically healed as the angels flew him through the gates of heaven.

"Want a line?" one of them asked, holding out a large tray of cocaine.

Dylan shrugged. "Why not?"

He snorted the drugs and glanced back at Jack, who was being dragged to hell by a pair of shrieking demons. Dylan felt some anger toward his boss for all he'd put him through. But mostly he was grateful to him. Because the old man was right—the job had taught him all he needed.

DINOSAUR

The dinosaur watched in silence as the younger writers took turns pitching jokes. They'd been at it for over an hour, shouting out punch lines at full voice. He hadn't seen a writers' room so animated since the eighties, back when everyone did cocaine.

"How about this?" suggested Surya, a twenty-four-year-old with purple hair. "Nimaah gets the Snapchat, turns to her girlfriend, and says, 'Woke up and smell the coffee.'"

Everyone laughed except the dinosaur. He made a mental note to look up the term "woke." This was the third time today someone had used it in a pitch. The dinosaur had no idea what it meant, although he'd come to believe it was somehow connected to Beyoncé. Was it a dance craze she had started? Like when Madonna did the vogue?

The dinosaur realized that some of the young human writers were peering up at him. He hadn't said anything since lunch, and his silence was growing conspicuous. A bead of sweat dribbled down his scaly green back. He had to contribute something.

"How about this?" he said, flicking his tiny dinosaur wrist in a show of nonchalance. "How about…someone says...'Roar...I'm a dinosaur...I'm gonna kill you with my mouth'?"

The room fell silent. Several writers took out their iPhones and pretended to check their email. The dinosaur could feel his tail wagging nervously behind him.

"Or, you know," he mumbled, "something *like* that. That was the bad version..." He lowered his giant dinosaur head. "Or maybe something with 'woke,'" he murmured softly. "Something where someone does the woke."

Cheryl, the showrunner, cleared her throat. "I think it might be time for a juice break," she said. The writers nodded solemnly and filed out the door. The dinosaur couldn't help but notice that nobody had offered to bring him back a juice. He didn't drink juice—he was a dinosaur—but still, it stung.

The dinosaur turned toward Cheryl. She was only about one-twentieth his size, but that didn't make her any less intimidating.

"Some really funny pitches back there!" said the dinosaur. "Surya's really bringing it today!"

"We need to talk," Cheryl said.

The dinosaur swallowed. He was trying his best to seem calm, but his wagging tail gave him away. It kept smashing into the corkboard, ripping note cards off the wall and sending pushpins flying through the air.

"Listen," Cheryl said. "I really appreciate all that you've brought to the room. Experience..." She closed her eyes for a beat, clearly trying to come up with another positive attribute. "Experience," she repeated. "But unfortunately, I just don't think this show is a good fit for you."

The dinosaur blinked his yellow eyes, trying his best to hold back tears. He'd been writing for TV for a hundred million years, and nothing like this had ever happened to him before.

"Look," he said. "I know my pitches have been kinda weak lately. But I swear I can get it together."

"It's not just that," Cheryl said quietly.

The dinosaur squinted at her. "What do you mean?"

Cheryl looked the dinosaur firmly in the eye. "You've been making the other writers feel unsafe."

The dinosaur laughed, his razor-sharp teeth glinting in the light. "Unsafe? What are you talking about?"

"Some of your pitches have crossed the line. For instance, the ones about killing people with your mouth."

The dinosaur folded his tiny arms and cocked his head. "I'm sorry," he said sarcastically. "I didn't realize we weren't allowed to pitch *jokes* in a *writers' room*."

"It's not just jokes," Cheryl said, her voice lowering. "On more than one occasion I've gotten complaints from human staffers that you've made them feel physically uncomfortable."

"Give me one example!" said the dinosaur. He bit his lip. He'd meant to speak in a professional tone of voice, but the statement had come out as more of a deafening roar.

Cheryl picked up her glasses, which had blown off her face, and coolly wiped the lenses with a tissue.

"Okay, fine," she said. "Last Friday, at drinks, someone said they saw you put your teeth around Marlyse's neck, like you were going to eat her. And then you roared and said, 'I'm gonna eat you. I'm a dinosaur!'"

"Are you serious?" the dinosaur said. "She's upset about that?"

Cheryl nodded. "The word she used was 'traumatized.'"

"That was just a bit!" the dinosaur protested. "At Letterman, we did stuff like that all the time!"

"Yeah, well, times have changed."

The dinosaur massaged his giant temples.

"Look," he said softly. "I'm sorry, all right? Please give me another chance. I need this job. My ex-wife is insane. She's a velociraptor, and believe me, the stereotypes are true. You know what she asked for in the settlement? My *meat*. She wants to literally, like, *take* chunks of my body and eat them, like food!"

He heard a distant peal of youthful laughter. The humans were returning with their juices.

"I guess I should head out," he murmured.

"I think that would be best," Cheryl said. "Good luck."

"Yeah," the dinosaur said, his voice slightly choked. "Thank you."

He couldn't fit through the door of the conference room so he walked through a brick wall, leaving behind a large dinosaur-shaped hole, one of many he had created during his tenure at the show. He looked through the hole from the sidewalk, wondering if it was the last time he'd ever get to see the inside of a writers' room. There was only one way to find out.

"I'm sorry," said the dinosaur's agent over the phone.

"Come on, Haiyan!" the dinosaur pleaded. "There's gotta be *something*!"

"I don't know what to tell you."

The dinosaur shook his head wearily. His original agent, Sol, had retired five years ago, and he'd never really jelled with the woman who replaced him. It had taken three days to get her to even return his frantic voicemails.

"What if I lowered my quote?" he asked. "I could work for a show as a story editor or a staff writer."

"The Writers Guild won't allow it," she said. "You're a dinosaur. You need to get paid dinosaur rates."

"What about my spec script?"

There was a long pause on the other end of the line.

"Hello?" said the dinosaur. "Haiyan, did I lose you?"

"I'm here," Haiyan said.

"What about my spec script?" the dinosaur repeated. "Did you send it out?"

"Yes," she said.

"That's great! What are people saying?"

Haiyan hesitated. "The response has been mixed."

The dinosaur's yellow eyes widened with shock. He'd never been more confident in a screenplay in his life. "That's crazy!" he said. "What don't people like about it?"

"The most common complaint we're getting is that the jokes seem a little dated."

"You mean the fax machine runner?"

"There's that," Haiyan acknowledged. "But also, a lot of the jokes tend to be about humans, and about how they're weaker than dinosaurs."

"They *are* weaker!" roared the dinosaur. "That's what's funny about them!"

There was a long silence. The dinosaur got the sense that at some point he'd been put on speakerphone.

"I'll let you know if anything comes up," Haiyan said curtly.

"Yeah, okay," said the dinosaur. "Thank you."

The dinosaur poured himself some scotch and glanced at the rusted Emmy Award on his mantel. He'd won it back in the Jurassic period, right before Letterman moved to CBS. At the time, he'd thought he'd be on top forever. He remembered a meeting he'd had with Sol, in which the old man had urged him to register his most popular sketch characters with the Writers Guild.

"Trust me," he'd said. "You'll want those residuals when you're an old has-been."

The paperwork had sat on the dinosaur's desk for two years, and eventually he'd thrown it out to make room for an espresso machine. How could he have been so naïve?

He lapped up some scotch with his tongue. It was strange: even though his career was in shambles, he didn't *feel* less talented than he used to be. He felt like the same old dinosaur. Gradually, a thought began to form in his walnut-sized brain: *Maybe it isn't my fault. Maybe society is to blame.*

He thought about his heroes: Lenny Bruce, George Carlin, Mel Brooks. You could never get away with stuff like that today. And why? Because of political correctness! *That* was the problem. The touchy-feely, namby-pamby liberals were destroying TV comedy. And it was up to the dinosaur to fix it.

The only question was: how? He could go on a crazy rampage, he supposed, and murder everyone by ripping them apart with his teeth and then eating their bones. But then everyone would say that *he* was the crazy one. There had to be a more elegant solution.

A soft blue light beckoned to him from across the room: the power button of his Dell computer. Of course! The answer was right in front of him! He patted his Emmy for good luck, then finished his scotch and started typing.

The dinosaur woke up the next morning with the worst headache of his life. He was groping around the medicine cabinet for some Tylenol with codeine when a hazy memory flashed through his mind.

He had written something.

He took a deep breath and reached for his BlackBerry. There was a rare missed call from Haiyan.

"How bad is it?" he asked her.

"Pretty bad," she said. "Look on Deadline."

The dinosaur squinted at his Dell. "How do I get to their website?"

Haiyan cursed with impatience. "Just type the word 'deadline' into Google and click on the first link."

"Okay, bear with me. I didn't learn touch-typing in school. Okay...almost there...Oh my God! 'Dinosaur posts hate screed on Facebook'? Does that mean me?"

"Yes."

"God damn it!"

The dinosaur put on his glasses and scrolled through the post. It was studded with boldfaced names, all of them celebrities who had condemned his rant on Twitter.

"This is crazy!" the dinosaur shouted into his phone. "How can I be 'prejudiced' if I myself am a minority?"

"What are you talking about?" Haiyan asked.

"I'm Jewish!"

"That doesn't count," Haiyan said.

The dinosaur roared.

"Listen," Haiyan said. "I'm sorry to do this over the phone. But I can no longer in good conscience represent you."

The dinosaur's mouth went dry. "What do you mean?"

"The agency is dropping you as a client," she said. "Take care of yourself."

The line went dead, and the dinosaur knew what it meant for his career. As quick as the flash of a comet, it was over.

• • •

It took almost a year for the dinosaur to find a job, but eventually he scored a gig bartending at an Irish pub in Studio City. It was tough on his ego at first, but as the years wore on, he grew to like the work. Nobody at Hallohan's knew about his past. He was just some dinosaur bringing them their Guinness.

A television was mounted in the corner of the bar. It was usually tuned to sports, but sometimes a sitcom would come on. The dinosaur would watch for a few minutes, trying to make sense of the references. He didn't think the shows were very funny. But if the customers seemed into it, he let them watch and even offered to turn up the volume.

He was mopping up some peanut crumbs one day when he heard someone call out his name. He looked up and saw a middle-aged Indian guy smiling at him.

"Sorry to bother you," he said, "but I think we used to work together."

The dinosaur squinted at the human, trying to place him. "I'm sorry," he said. "My memory sucks."

The customer smiled sheepishly. "I used to have purple hair," he said.

The dinosaur laughed with excitement. It was Surya, the staff writer he'd worked with on his very last TV show. He poured out a scotch and slid it across the bar. "Drink up!" he said. "It's on the house!"

Surya thanked the dinosaur and filled him in on the past two decades. He'd risen in the ranks, all the way up to showrunner. The dinosaur felt a stab of jealousy, but it passed. "That's great, Surya," he said. "I always knew you had it in you."

Surya thanked him, but the dinosaur could sense some weariness in his voice. He poured him another drink. "What's up?" he asked.

"I don't know," Surya said. "It's my staff. It's difficult to connect with them."

"Are they funny?"

"I have no idea," Surya admitted. "All of them are robots, and their references are crazy. It's always 'terabyte' this and 'gigabyte' that." A few customers glanced at Surya, clearly offended by his robot impression. He hung his head with shame.

The dinosaur slid him a bowl of peanuts. "Just make sure to register your characters with the Writers Guild. Trust me, you'll want those residuals."

"That's good advice," Surya said. "Thank you."

The dinosaur bashfully flicked his little arm. "It's nothing."

"I'm serious," Surya said. "You're saving my life here."

The dinosaur grinned. "Usually, with dinosaurs, it's the other way around."

The line was so tasteless Surya couldn't help but laugh.

"Oh man," he said as bits of peanut sprayed out of his mouth. "You got me."

The dinosaur tried to respond, but his voice got caught in his throat. He gave a slight bow, then grabbed a rag and gratefully wiped up the crumbs.

ARTIST'S REVENGE

Michael Dane knew that, objectively, his directing career had been successful.

His movies had grossed more than three billion dollars. They'd spawned video games, comic books, restaurants, Macy's floats, and theme parks. When he released a new sequel, people camped out for days for a chance to see it early. He was friends with Johnny Depp. Not close friends, but definitely legitimately friends, like they texted each other funny links and stuff.

But despite all his accomplishments, he couldn't help but feel like a failure. And the reason was simple: Alan Schwab.

For decades, the legendary film critic had dogged him, describing his work as "cheap," "hollow," "flimsy," and "disgusting." Lately, he'd even begun to insult Dane in reviews of other people's work, referring to choices that upset him as "Dane-esque."

In interviews, Dane claimed he "never read reviews." But secretly, Schwab's words were seared into his brain. Every night, while he tried to fall asleep in his large glass mansion with an unobstructed view of the ocean, Dane thought of Schwab's cruelty. How could he get back at him? How could he even the score? Revenge seemed impossible. But then one night, like so many times in his career, it happened: inspiration.

Alan Schwab woke up naked in an underground bunker, his arms and legs chained to a chair.

"Don't move," Dane whispered from the shadows. "You're still recovering from major surgery."

The critic looked down and gasped. Sure enough, there was a jagged incision just below his nipple.

"My God!" he cried. "What's happening?"

"An explosive device has been implanted in your chest," Dane continued. "If you don't do exactly as I say, I will detonate your heart." He stepped slowly into the light, holding a small remote control. "You might recognize this gambit from my film *Final Battle 2*. In your review, you called it an 'overly simplistic plot contrivance.' Well, as you can see, it gets the job done."

"What do you want?" Schwab begged.

Dane handed the critic a piece of paper and whipped out a small, sleek camera.

"Look into the lens," he said. "And read your lines."

Alan was about to comply when Dane held up his palm. Despite the circumstances, he was still a director, and he couldn't resist giving a couple of notes.

"Try to deliver the lines with some joy," he said. "Your motivation is 'to reassure.'"

Alan nodded awkwardly.

"Okay," the director whispered. "Action."

"This is Alan Schwab," the critic said. "I have decided to take a one-year leave of absence from writing reviews in order to pursue my secret lifelong dream: to direct a movie of my own."

"Cut," said the director, turning off the camera. "Nice work, really natural. I think we got it."

Alan looked at his captor with confusion. "What happens now?"

Dane giddily explained the rules. Schwab would have one year to complete a feature film. If he failed, refused, or told anybody the circumstances, his torso would explode. Other than those basic stipulations, though, Schwab would enjoy complete creative freedom. He could work in any style or genre that he pleased. Regardless of content or length, Schwab's film would be given a full theatrical release with his name in giant letters on the poster.

"You'll get all the credit," Dane explained, "positive or negative."

He took out a gem-studded Montblanc pen (a prop from *Final Battle 4: The Final Battle*) and scribbled out a check for thirty million dollars.

"Here you go," he said, pressing the check into Schwab's hand. "That's a big enough budget to hire Meryl Streep."

Schwab winced as the bunker doors slid open, flooding his eyes with California sunlight.

"Now it's your turn," the director told him. "Now *you* go make a fucking movie."

• • •

Dane flew east in his private jet, his face suffused with pleasure. In his lap was an iPad opened to a recent post on Deadline. He'd put off reading it for several hours, to better savor the experience, but he couldn't hold out any longer. He picked up the tablet and scrolled through the paragraphs, pausing after each, like he did when eating *uni* rolls at Masa.

Schwab Film in Trouble, Sources Say

One year ago, esteemed critic Alan Schwab shocked the film community by publicly declaring his ambition to direct a film himself. From day one, expectations were sky-high. Schwab is considered one of the world's foremost authorities on film, and cinephiles everywhere assumed his work would be up to his own high standards. However, as production comes to a close, Schwab's project is rumored to be struggling, with some on-set sources calling it "a scary situation."

"He cries all the time," said one crew member, who spoke to me on the condition of anonymity. "And whenever somebody asks him a question, like how to block a scene or what shot he wants next, he falls to his knees and starts whispering, 'I can't take it anymore.' That's usually when he passes out one of his weird notes."

Schwab's handwritten notes are becoming something of a legend on the lot. I've been shown several, and even by the standards of feature directors, the letters are eccentric. They always begin in the same way, with a plea for the recipient to "not say anything" because he's "probably being watched." He then pleads with them to "find a surgeon" to "silently operate on his chest" and "take out the detonator in [his] chest."

It's unclear what's happening to Schwab. Some of my sources theorize that the pressures of directing have caused him to have a psychotic breakdown. Others are more charitable.

"It's a little unusual to pass out notes like that," said one studio veteran. "I mean, for a director to beg the crew to operate on his body, that's definitely strange. But compared to David O. Russell? It's not that shocking."

Experts agree that if this were a studio venture, Schwab would have been removed from the feature long ago. But his independent financier, who continues to remain anonymous, has vowed to stick with the newbie director, no matter what.

"We wholeheartedly believe in Alan Schwab's vision," wrote the unknown benefactor in a recent online statement, "and we are excited to share that vision with the world."

Schwab's film, *Help Me, There's a Bomb in My Chest, I'm Not Pitching Titles, This Is Real!*, will premiere tomorrow at the Cannes Film Festival.

Dane gazed out the window as the sandy French shore came into view. He had fallen behind on his latest Final Battle sequel (*Final Battle 5: Armistice*). But he felt no desire to work on the script. His masterpiece was already in progress.

Three hundred reporters looked on curiously as Alan Schwab took the stage to introduce his film. He was dressed like a typical first-time director, in a slightly rumpled, rented black tuxedo. But there were clues that something was amiss. His eyes were bloodshot, as if he hadn't slept in days, and his forehead was coated with sweat. He was also accompanied by a man in a black face mask, who stood silently beside him, holding what looked like a bomb detonator.

"This is a real movie," Schwab began, shooting nervous glances at the masked man. "I made it by choice." He covered his face with his hands and gave himself over to a lengthy crying jag. "I'm scared," he murmured finally. "I'm scared."

The audience awkwardly applauded as the lights began to dim.

"I can't take this anymore," Schwab whimpered to his captor as they stood in the wings. "Just kill me. Kill me!"

"Not a chance," Dane said. "You're going to live through this experience. You're going to see what it's like to step into the arena and fail before the throngs. To get a taste of your own medicine, a sip of your own—"

He'd prepared several pages of this sort of dialogue, but before he could finish reciting it all, he became aware of a disconcerting sound.

Applause.

• • •

Dane flew west in his private jet, his face suffused with pain. His iPad sat on his lap, opened to a recent post on Deadline. It wasn't easy, but after several hours, he forced himself to scroll through the paragraphs.

Alan Schwab Dazzles Cannes
with Experimental Masterpiece

Once in a generation a film emerges with so much daring it threatens to disrupt the entire medium. *Help Me, There's a Bomb in My Chest, I'm Not Pitching Titles, This Is Real!* may be such a film.

At fourteen minutes, *Help Me* is short by the standards of most feature films. But don't let the running time fool you. Alan Schwab's film contains more ingenuity than all the studio releases of the past ten years combined.

The film opens with a haunting image. An unnamed woman (played with graceful understatement by Meryl Streep) stands in the middle of what appears to be a Hollywood soundstage. A frightened man, played by Schwab himself, runs over to her and presses a note into her hands.

"Help me," he whispers. "There's a bomb in my chest. Oh God, help me."

The shot ends abruptly—with a swift cut to black.

The rest of the film consists of variations on this theme. Again and again, Schwab's "frightened man" character approaches people, desperately begging for help and demanding that they perform surgery on his body to "remove the bomb" or "get rid of the bomb." Sometimes, we hear his cries offscreen. Occasionally, he stares right into camera, as if asking us, the audience, to assist him.

"There's a bomb in my chest," he tells us as tears stream down his ashen, haunted face. "This isn't made-up. I don't want to direct this movie. I'm doing it because someone put a bomb in my chest and he threatened me. I'm afraid to say his name because he'll kill me. Oh God, help me. I'm so scared. I need surgery to remove the bomb from my chest!"

One hopes that Schwab will remove more from his chest. More honesty, more emotion, more art. The world would be a richer place for it.

Does *Help Me, There's a Bomb in My Chest, I'm Not Pitching Titles, This Is Real!* have its flaws? Of course. The film can feel repetitive at times, given the fact that so much of the dialogue consists of the same few phrases said over and over again (most notably "Help me" and "There's a bomb inside my chest"). But these are minor quibbles. If you like your films slick and sanitized, you can go to your local multiplex and watch the latest offering from Michael Dane.

Or, like Schwab, you can take a risk. You can see Schwab's film, open up *your* chest, and see the human heart beating inside.

Michael Dane powered down his iPad. Then, for the first time in his life, he considered the option of suicide. He didn't have any weapons in his jet. Although his gem-studded Montblanc fountain pen was reasonably sharp. He took it out of his pocket and stared at its glistening nib. He wondered what it would look like to see it slash into his wrist.

It would be pretty cool-looking, actually. Especially if you scored it with some dubstep and shot it at a hundred frames a second. He could see the parabolic arc of blood, rising and falling out of frame. It could be the opening shot of a major battle.

Perhaps even a Final Battle.

He pressed the pen nib lightly to his wrist and carefully wrote himself a note:

Final Battle 5 intro shot—pen slash?

It was only a start, but it had potential. He'd figure out the rest when he got back to Los Angeles. He couldn't wait to land. He was Michael Dane, God damn it, and he had work to do.

STAGE 13

Yoni was haunted by his student loan debt. He felt its weight whenever he purchased a granola bar or fed quarters into a washing machine. As of this morning, he owed $97,201.83. And the worst part was, he'd spent it all on nothing.

Since graduating from film school seven years ago, Yoni's filmmaking career had gone from promising to catastrophic. He'd managed to direct a few dog food commercials, but the best he could say about them was that, from a legal standpoint, the animals had not been abused. His nondog work was similarly bleak: Hardee's training videos, infomercials designed to trick the elderly, and workout DVDs for exercise programs that were at best a scam and at worst medically dangerous.

Yoni knew his best hope was to move back into his parents' house in Queens. His mother had befriended the owner of a successful mulch business, and according to her frequent emails, there was a job "with his name on it." Yoni wasn't sure what his role at the mulch business would be. Making it, selling it, spreading it? But anything was better than staying in Los Angeles, chasing a dream he knew was dead. He was thirty-four years old. If things were going to happen for him, they would've happened by now.

Yoni was browsing some cheap flights back east when his cracked iPhone buzzed in his pocket. He squinted at the unknown number. He knew he should ignore the call; it was almost certainly a debt collection agency. But the 323 area code gave him pause. Whoever was calling him was calling from Hollywood itself. His phone rang a third time, then a fourth, then a fifth. It was about to go to voicemail when Yoni cursed at himself under his breath and answered.

"I'm glad you could make it," said Nikki Coleman, an elegantly dressed executive of indeterminate age. "Was parking all right?"

Yoni nodded enthusiastically, even though he'd come by Lyft. It was the first time he'd ever been invited to a major movie studio. He had no idea how Paragon had gotten his number and was almost positive they had contacted him as the result of some administrative error. Still, he was determined to make a good impression.

"I'll cut to the chase," Nikki said as her handsome assistant handed Yoni an impressively cold bottle of Fiji water. "The reason I called is because we've been watching your work for some time, and we're considering hiring you for a major project."

Several seconds passed in silence.

"Like, a directing thing?" Yoni asked.

"Yes," Nikki said patiently. "A directing thing."

Yoni shook his head in disbelief. "What made you think of me?"

Nikki smiled as broadly as she could, given her many facial surgeries. "We've had some problems on set," she said. "I won't go into specifics right now. But we need someone with experience working with unconventional talent."

Yoni nodded. If there was one skill he had, it was dealing with temperamental stars. He'd once directed a workout tape starring a bodybuilder who was addicted, in his own words, to "rage."

"Who is it?" he whispered. It was his first taste of industry gossip, and he was excited. "Is it Bale?"

Nikki nodded subtly at her assistant, who held up a giant stack of paper.

"Before I can tell you about the project," Nikki said, "I need you to sign a nondisclosure agreement."

Yoni flipped through the baffling pile of pages. "What does this all mean, exactly?"

"It's just standard boilerplate," Nikki assured him. "All it says is that you'll keep everything you hear and see today a secret, no matter how shocking or horrific."

"Huh," Yoni said. He thought about his options and then neatly signed the contract. "So... what happens now?"

Nikki's eyes narrowed. "You meet her."

Yoni sat in the passenger seat of Nikki's golf cart as she sped them through the lot. He recognized some of the sets from movies—the police station from a car chase franchise, the haunted graveyard from a recent thriller. Gradually, though, as they drove through the studio, the sets grew less familiar.

They passed a dated mock-up of a subway station, covered in 1980s-style graffiti, then a decrepit Wild West set. It was another ten minutes before the cart came to a stop.

"Here we are," Nikki said. "Stage 13."

Yoni climbed out of the golf cart and followed Nikki over to a barren concrete structure. The other soundstages they'd passed, Yoni noticed, had golden plaques affixed to their front doors, commemorating the films that had been shot there. Stage 13, in contrast, was eerily unmarked. The grass outside had been neglected, and the crumbling wooden door creaked open as they neared it, as if pushed by some knowing, spectral force.

"So," Yoni asked cautiously, "what's the deal here?"

Nikki dispassionately summarized the building's history. The stage was built in 1914 to produce silent one-reelers. It thrived for a couple of years, producing racist but profitable hits, like *Hong Kong Harry*. Sometime in the twenties, though, it began to acquire a "negative reputation." A 1926 ice-skating musical was shut down in the middle of production due to a catastrophic freezer explosion. Since then, the stage had been the site of numerous violent accidents: fallen lights, snapped riggings, mysterious electrical fires. After World War II, the stage fell into disuse. It was revived in the 1950s for a Christmas movie, but the film was abandoned when the director went insane and demanded to be given a lobotomy.

"And this is where I would be working?" Yoni asked.

"Yes," Nikki said.

Yoni nodded. It was at times like these that he wished he belonged to some kind of union.

"After you," Nikki said.

Yoni took a deep breath and stepped into the darkened soundstage. He was searching in vain for a light switch when a sparkling figure burst into view overhead, as bright as an antique camera flash. By the time Yoni regained his vision, the glittering presence was floating down toward him from the ceiling. She was slightly translucent, with sunken eyes and fiery red hair.

"What's that?" Yoni asked.

"That's Clara," Nikki said. "She's a ghost."

Yoni had some follow-up questions, but before he could ask them, Nikki bolted for the exit, slamming the heavy door behind her.

Yoni turned reluctantly toward Clara. At some point she had floated down to eye level. He could feel her cold breath on his face.

"Hi," he said uneasily. "My name's Yoni."

Her bloodred lips curled into a smile. "The new director," she said.

"Yep!" Yoni said, smiling brightly to conceal his mounting terror. "It's nice to meet you."

He held out his hand, and she shook it to the best of her ability, her translucent fingers passing through his flesh.

"Cool!" Yoni said. "Cool, cool." He could see Clara better now. She didn't look like a traditional Hollywood actress. But her face was certainly captivating: sunken eyes, long black lashes, ghoulishly white skin. Yoni couldn't tell how much of her aesthetic was a personal style choice and how much a result of her being dead. In either case, it worked; Yoni couldn't take his eyes off her.

"How long have you been here?" he asked.

"Since 1922," she said. "I was over for a screen test. It was my seventh audition in three days, and I was pretty hopped up on reds. Guess I took too many. Anyway, I passed out and cracked my head over there."

She pointed at a faded red stain on the concrete.

Yoni winced. "Did it hurt?"

Clara shook her head. "I fell right asleep. And when I woke up, there's this tall, golden man staring down at me. And he tells me it's time to leave this world behind. 'Sweet child,' he says. 'You've been struggling so long. Striving and suffering. It's made us angels weep. But be not afraid. Soon you will be in the warm embrace of God, and all your pain will cease to be. Come, my darling child, and bask in the light of heaven.' So I stand up and look into his big golden eyes. And I say, 'Bullshit. I'm not leaving this town until I'm a fucking star.' So he smiles down at me and says, 'Be at peace, my child. Fame and success are but man-made idols. And once thou art in heaven, thou shalt learn there's no such thing as worldly glory, for in God's eyes, all creatures are made equal.' And I say, 'If I wanted to be equal, I would have stayed in Galveston, Texas. I have a screen test in two hours to play the ingénue in a one-reeler, and if you make me miss it, I swear I'm going to kill you.' And he reaches out and takes my hand and starts to lift me up off the ground, to heaven or wherever. So I take out my hairpin and I stab him as hard as I can in his wing. Just stab him and stab him and stab him. And he can't feel pain because he's an angel, but eventually he's like, 'Stop. That's annoying.' And I say, 'I'm gonna stab you all the way up to heaven unless you let me go!' And he says, 'You're crazy, Pamela.' And I say, "My name's Clara Ginger now. I changed it to look better on marquees. Tell God and everyone to stop calling me Pamela. I'm not Pamela anymore. It's Clara Ginger, damn it!' And I keep stabbing him in the wing and the face. And eventually he loses his cool and drops the whole goody-two-shoes bit and says, 'You're one crazy bitch.' So I look him in his golden eyes and say, 'You can eat my ass.'" She chuckled proudly at the memory. "Anyway. Since then I've been here."

Clara walked Yoni through her present circumstances. She couldn't leave the soundstage ("standard ghost rules"), but she had a lot of power within its crumbling walls. "I can move stuff with my mind and fly around and shit. Comes in handy when people piss me off. But after a while, believe me, it gets old."

The worst part, she said, was that God probably thought he was "winning."

"I bet he's looking down on me right now," she said. "Laughing on top of some dumb cloud." She put her hands on her hips and launched into a God impression. "Oooooooh, I'm God. I don't think Clara's *ever* gonna be in pictures..."

Yoni glanced nervously toward the sky as Clara continued her impression of the Lord. Her God voice had started off as only subtly gay, but as she spoke, it grew more aggressively flamboyant.

"Oooh, I'm God, sitting around with my tutti-frutti angels..."

"Clara."

"...getting fucked in the butt all the time..."

"Whoa."

Clara flicked her wrist. "Relax. There's nothing he can do."

"It seems like there's a lot he can do," Yoni cautioned. "I mean, he turned you into a ghost."

"Big whoop. I'm still gonna be a star."

"How?"

"You're the director," she said. "You figure it out."

"We've tried everything to get rid of her," Nikki explained as Yoni climbed back into the golf cart. "Mediums, exorcists, sage spells. Nothing works. She just gets mad and starts killing people."

Yoni nodded. "She seems pretty determined to make it as an actress."

"We've consulted with several ghost experts," Nikki said. "Clara won't go to heaven until she's accomplished what she sees as her 'unfinished business on this earth.'"

"I'm sure I can find something to direct her in," Yoni said. "I mean, makeup will be a challenge, but I'll figure it out."

"It's not that simple," Nikki said. "We can't reveal Clara's existence to the world."

Yoni nodded. "Mankind would panic if they learned that ghosts were real."

"There's that," Nikki acknowledged. "But mainly, it's a liability issue. By concealing Clara's existence all these years, Paragon Studios has enabled countless deaths. According to our lawyers, the class action potential is significant."

"How can you keep Clara a secret and make her a movie star at the same time?"

Nikki parked her golf cart in front of an unmarked storage unit. "I'll show you."

A musty smell hit Yoni's nose as he followed her into the cramped storage locker. He was starting to feel claustrophobic when the fluorescents flickered on overhead. Instantaneously, his anxiety gave way to childlike wonder. He was surrounded by ancient film equipment dating back to the silent era.

"You'd be working with this crap," Nikki said, gesturing at a hand-crank camera, plated with silver and gold.

Yoni laughed with geeky amazement. "Holy shit! Is that a Bell and Howell?"

Nikki shrugged.

"I think this is what Chaplin used!" Yoni said, patting the old machine with reverence. "I can't believe this thing still works!"

"It doesn't," Nikki said. "There isn't even a lens." She jabbed her finger through the hollow cylinder. "See?"

"So how am I going to shoot with it?" Yoni asked.

"You're not."

Yoni's posture slumped as the situation dawned on him. "So you don't actually want me to direct anything. You just want me to pretend to direct something. So you can trick a ghost."

Nikki nodded. "Is that a problem?"

"I mean, it's a little disappointing." He looked up at her with hope in his eyes. "Unless you think this project might lead to something! Like, if I did a good job, do you think you might consider me for other jobs? Like, directing real movies, without ghosts?"

"We see this as more of a one-off gig," she said.

Yoni gave a disappointed nod.

"Look," Nikki said. "It's easy work. All you have to do is point the camera at Clara for a few hours. We'll hire some nonunion crew to run around and look busy. She'll sashay around, you'll spin the crank, and then a week later I'll come in with a fake copy of *Variety*. 'Clara Ginger is a star.' She'll see the headline, fly up to heaven, and that'll be that."

"What would I tell her she's starring in?"

Nikki handed him a script, and he read the title out loud. "*Mr. Ching Chong and the Orphan Girl?*"

Nikki nodded. "It's the one-reeler Clara was auditioning for the day she died. Fun fact: it was considered racist even for its time."

"I'm not sure I can do this," Yoni said. "I mean, it doesn't seem very creatively fulfilling. Also, I'm concerned that

Clara would find out I was tricking her and then murder me."

"If you get her to leave," Nikki said, "we'll pay you one hundred thousand dollars."

Yoni picked up the camera and tested out the crank.

Yoni stood outside the soundstage, waiting for his crew to finish signing their confidentiality agreements. Nikki had briefed them about Clara, but they still were understandably afraid. Yoni cleared his throat and launched into a pep talk.

"Okay!" he said. "So we're about to go inside, to encounter the ghost we're attempting to trick. It's going to be weird, but we're gonna get through it. Does anyone have any questions?"

A handsome, out-of-work actor named Charles raised his hand. Yoni recognized him vaguely from a local commercial for yard furniture.

"Is this makeup really necessary?" he asked.

Yoni nodded at Charles sympathetically. "Unfortunately, the part of Mr. Ching Chong calls for full yellow-face makeup. If you don't wear it, Clara will get suspicious."

Charles shut his eyes. "This is rock-bottom for me," he said to no one in particular. "Playing a racist caricature to trick a ghost."

Yoni could tell the day would be an uphill battle. But what was the alternative? He pictured himself declaring bankruptcy and flying back to Queens to join the mulch trade. He could see his parents standing on the porch, his mother sobbing with relief, his father savoring his vindication.

"So it didn't work out in Lala Land," he could hear him saying. *"Well, at least you're finally back on Planet Earth."*

Yoni knew his film career was over. But with a hundred grand, he could at least avoid that nightmarish homecoming. He could pay off his debt, flee LA forever, and start a new life somewhere else, doing anything but this.

He opened the door and led the crew into the darkened soundstage. A few men screamed as Clara floated into view. In general, though, they managed to remain professional-looking.

"Who are all these guys?" Clara asked suspiciously.

Yoni bounded toward her and held up a copy of the script. "Congratulations!" he said. "You got the part!"

"Which part?"

Yoni grinned. "The lead!"

"Bullshit," Clara spat, her pupils burning like a pair of embers. "This is some kind of trick, and I'm going to murder *everybody!*"

Yoni swallowed. He could hear one of the crew members behind him vomit with fear.

"It's no trick!" Yoni assured her. He pulled out his Bell and Howell. "See?"

Clara's jaw was clenched with rage. But when she saw the gleaming camera, her expression softened. She inched toward the machine and peered into the lens-less aperture,

212

her lips slowly parting. When she looked up, her eyes were wide and hopeful.

"I'm really the lead?" she asked in a small voice.

"Yeah!" Yoni said. "Big-time!"

A tear rolled down Clara's pale cheek. Within seconds, though, she'd suppressed any trace of vulnerability.

"Well then, shit, what are we waiting for?" she said. "Let's get to work."

The plot of *Mr. Ching Chong and the Orphan Girl* wasn't particularly complicated. An orphan girl visits the shop of Mr. Ching Chong to pawn her beloved silver locket. Mr. Ching Chong tries to cheat her, but she hypnotizes him with the locket and gets him to jump out the window. The rest of the nine-page scenario called for Clara to face the camera and cycle through a series of popular 1920s dance crazes, none of which had any relation to the story.

Yoni explained to Clara that they were going to shoot the movie in one take. It all took place on a single set, so continuity wouldn't be an issue. Furthermore, since the film was silent, there was no need to learn or practice any lines.

"We can start right now," he said cheerfully. "And we'll be finished in under ten minutes."

Clara looked worried. "Shouldn't we rehearse a little first?" she asked. "Or at least block it?"

If this were a real film, Yoni would pull his star aside to reassure her. But given the circumstances, he didn't see the need.

"Don't worry," he said to Clara. "You're gonna nail it."

He checked to make sure that the camera was pointed in the right direction. Then he spun the crank around and called out, "Action!"

Clara pointed at the locket and held her hands together in a pleading gesture.

"Great acting!" Yoni said. "Let's move on to the hypnotizing part."

Clara swung the locket back and forth. Charles dutifully jumped out the window.

"Great!" Yoni said. "Let's wrap it up."

Clara turned to the camera and energetically cycled through her dances: the Mexican Tamale, the Irish Jig, and the Jewish Shuffle.

"Wow," Yoni said involuntarily. "Okay! Great work, Clara. That's a wrap."

Clara looked around the room as the crew members silently dispersed. "Really?" she asked. "That's it?"

Yoni gave her two thumbs-up. "That's it!"

Clara looked down at her feet.

"What's wrong?" Yoni asked.

She gestured at the crew. "They hated it."

Yoni forced a laugh. "What are you talking about?" he said. "They loved it! Right, guys?"

The crew members nodded fearfully.

"Don't fuck with me!" Clara shouted at Yoni. "It fucking died and you know it!"

Yoni fell backward as she flew up to the ceiling and

slipped into the shadows. The air was so cold he could see his own breath. At this rate, he knew, Clara wasn't going anywhere.

Yoni spent the lunch break trying to teach his crew to feign praise more believably. But no matter how loudly they applauded, Yoni knew it wouldn't persuade Clara. She was a performer. And anyone who's ever been on-stage can tell when they've lost the crowd. It was something you could physically feel—the knot in your lungs, the sweat on your neck, the gnawing panic in your gut.

There was only one way to convince Clara that her film was working.

Somehow he would have to make it work.

He opened his battered laptop. His desktop was crawl-ing with Final Draft and QuickTime files, each icon a gravestone commemorating some failed project. There were the feature scripts he'd labored on in screenwriting class, including the earnest war epic his professor had called a "decent first attempt at comedy." There was the self-financed short he'd paid to submit to the Sundance Contest, a cruel scam with no affiliation whatsoever with the Sundance Film Festival. There were hundreds of storyboards, pitches, and treatments for movies that never were produced and never would be. And now here he was, writing a fake starring vehicle for a ghost. His only solace was that it was the last project he would ever work on, the last time he would ever have to type out those two conniving words that built up your hopes only to dash them:

Open on…

"Clara?" Yoni called. "You in here?"

Clara descended reluctantly from the ceiling. Her little jaw was locked and cocked in a way that reminded Yoni of a baby lion. He could tell from her streaked mascara she'd been crying.

"I'm sorry it didn't go well yesterday."

Clara shrugged. "It was just a little hiccup," she said. "Just another hurdle to jump over." She gazed off into the distance. "I remember when I entered my first dance contest. Miss Bathing Beauty, 1917. My act bombed in rehearsal. But that didn't stop me."

Yoni nodded. "You rehearsed."

Clara shook her head. "I screwed one of the judges. His name was Lou Dunlap. He owned a sauerkraut company, and his beard smelled like rotten cabbage. But I didn't care. I did things to him that would shock the devil. Things that would make the devil say, 'Whoa, that's enough. You don't have to take it that far. Slow down. That's crazy. Stop.' But I'll tell you what: it won me Miss Bathing Beauty. And the whole thing was worth it to prove them wrong."

"Prove who wrong?"

"Everyone," she said. "My teachers, my cousins, the nuns. They all used to laugh when they caught me practicing my walks in the mirror. Said I'd never amount to nothing. Well, look at me now. They're sitting on some dumb, fat cloud with God. And I'm in Los Angeles, living my dreams." She blinked away some tears. "You know what I mean?"

Yoni nodded, thinking of the people who had doubted him over the years: his mother, his father, his professors, his classmates, contest judges, YouTube commentators, that busboy he'd caught smirking at his laptop that one time when he was working on a screenplay at Chipotle, his guidance counselor, his college adviser, his unemployment officer, his therapist, the Barnes & Noble cashier who had sold him his copy of *Save the Cat!,* and sometimes, if he was being honest, himself.

He took out a packet of pages.

"What's that?" she asked.

"I took a new pass at the script," he said.

Clara squinted at the first page. "What kind of name is John for a Chinaman?"

"The shopkeeper's no longer Chinese."

"Then what kind of foreigner *is* he?"

"He's not a foreigner," Yoni said. "The script is no longer racist."

She telekinetically flung the script into a trash can.

"Can I at least pitch it to you?" he asked.

Clara sighed. "Fine."

"Okay," Yoni said. "So you know how the previous draft was a hateful attack against Chinese people?"

Clara nodded.

"Well, this version is more about two people coming together to achieve their dream."

"What's their dream?"

Yoni looked into her eyes. "To prove everyone wrong."

Yoni supervised the crew as they re-dressed the pawnshop set, transforming it into a cobbler's empty storefront. Charles, looking more confident without his yellow-face makeup, took his mark behind the cash register.

"Okay?" Yoni asked. "Is everybody ready?"

The crew shrugged.

"Clara?"

Clara shot an anxious glance at the crew, then turned to her director and nodded.

"Great!" Yoni said. "Action on rehearsal! Clara, you enter the shoe shop. And remember, you have a limp."

Clara entered the set, heavily dragging her left foot.

"That's great," Yoni said. "Okay, Charles, remember, your shoe shop is really struggling. You're sorting through your bills. How are you going to pay off all your debts? Big sigh. But then you look up and you see her. And you recognize her! She's that famous ballerina whose leg got run over by a trolley!"

Charles pointed at Clara in a show of enthusiasm.

"Good!" Yoni said. "You say that you're a fan. You praise a move you saw her do onstage. A special pirouette."

Charles did a clumsy spin.

"Nice," Yoni said. "Okay now, Clara, you don't want to

talk about your dancing days. It's too sad to think about your accident and all your thwarted dreams."

Clara turned her back to Charles and huffily headed for the door.

"Perfect," Yoni said. "It's still raining outside, but you don't care. You're getting out of this shop..."

Clara reached for the door handle.

"Okay!" Yoni shouted. "Now, Charles, you have an idea! You grab one of your shoes and beg her to try it on! Clara, you don't want to listen. You think he's crazy. You try to get away. But, Charles, you won't let her—you grab her foot! You stick the shoe on her foot!"

The crew members watched as Charles followed the instructions, grasping at Clara's calf as she kicked at him with a realistic blend of fear and outrage.

"You finally get the shoe on!" Yoni continued. "Clara, you're furious. You want to run away. But as you flee for the door, you notice something—your limp is gone! The shoe fixed it!"

Clara swiveled around and walked gracefully toward Charles, looking convincingly amazed.

"Yes!" Yoni said. "You can walk again! Just like in the old days! But can you dance? Is it possible? There's only one way to find out. You try the move he remembered—your special pirouette!"

Clara took a deep breath and twirled across the shop, her arms arced high over her head, her feet gliding through the sawdust. Charles stretched out his hands, and she landed in his arms, laughing with delight. Then her eyes filled with tears and she began sobbing, overcome with relief at the shocking resurrection of her dreams.

"Okay!" Yoni said. "Cut on rehearsal!"

He glanced at the crew. Instead of dispersing, they remained where they stood, their eyes on Clara.

Yoni turned to his star, and the two of them shared a subtle, victorious smile.

Nikki blinked slowly. "What do you mean 'new version'?"

"We've totally revamped the picture," Yoni reported. "And I really think it's got a chance of working."

Nikki nodded. "You think it will get Clara to stop haunting us."

"I actually meant, like, I think it works creatively. Like, as a piece of art."

Nikki's forehead twitched. "What?"

"You should see Clara in this thing," Yoni said. "She's a star."

"She's a ghost."

"The public doesn't have to know that! We can shoot her from low angles, to hide the fact she's floating."

"Yoni—"

"Just let me pitch it to you."

He fanned out his palms. "Okay," he said. *"Open on . . ."*

He quickly walked her through it—the characters, the story, the scoring, tone, and shooting style. He'd never been great at presenting his ideas, but as he spoke, his confidence grew. By the time he finished, he realized he was standing up, his arms raised in triumph.

"And that's the final shot!" he said. "They spin out of frame as we fade—no, cut! We *cut* to black."

He smiled hopefully at Nikki. At some point her forehead had stopped twitching.

"It wouldn't cost much," Yoni pleaded. "All we'd have to do, really, is put a working lens into the camera. What do you think?"

"I think," she said, "that you guys might be onto something."

Yoni grinned. "Really?"

Nikki stood up abruptly at her desk. "I want you to mock up a preliminary shooting schedule," she said. "It'll give me a better sense of what kind of budget we'll need."

"Of course!" Yoni said. "Absolutely!"

"Email it to me by nine a.m. tomorrow," she said. "In the meantime, I'll meet with marketing and distribution." She stopped at the door and looked over her shoulder. "Congratulations, Yoni. You pulled it off."

Yoni waited until the door was closed, then pumped his fist in triumph.

Yoni knew he should go straight home and get to work. But halfway to the studio gates, he stopped and turned around. He couldn't leave without telling Clara the good news.

He opened the door to Stage 13 and startled at the sight

of her. She was standing in the center of a golden shaft of light, an oddly placid smile on her face.

"Clara?" he asked. "What's going on?"

Nikki stepped out from the shadows. There was panic in her eyes, but she managed to quickly suppress it. "I was just telling Clara the good news," she said brightly.

Yoni noticed that Clara was holding a copy of *Variety*. He winced as he read the front-page headline.

CLARA GINGER SHINES IN MR. CHING CHONG AND THE ORPHAN GIRL!

The newspaper was obviously fake: the pages were printed on computer paper. But somehow the prop had managed to trick Clara.

"Isn't it amazing, Yoni?" she said as she elevated slowly toward the ceiling. "I had no idea the studio even released it!"

"Of course we released it," Nikki said, smiling up at the levitating spirit. "How could we not? It isn't often you see such a star-making performance."

"You can't leave!" Yoni shouted. "What about our new version of the movie?"

Clara smiled down at Yoni as her body continued to ascend. "I'm sorry," she said. "I couldn't stay even if I wanted to."

"Why not?"

She shrugged. "Standard ghost rules. My unfinished business on this earth is finished. I'm finally a star and now my soul is *free*."

Yoni watched as a halo began to form around her head.

The circle was almost complete when he shouted up at her. "Clara, wait!"

Clara opened her eyes and smiled down beatifically. "What's up?"

"There's something you need to know."

Nikki turned to Yoni in wide-eyed disbelief. "Yoni!" she hissed. "Are you fucking crazy? Stop!"

"That magazine is fake," Yoni continued.

Clara sunk down a couple of inches. "Excuse me?"

Yoni heard a door slam shut. At some point Nikki had fled the soundstage, leaving him alone with the ghost.

He cleared his throat and kept going.

"I'm sorry," he said. "The whole thing was a trick."

"I don't believe you," she said, shaking her head. "Prove it!"

Yoni held up the lens-less camera, took a deep breath, and stuck his finger through the hollow aperture. Clara began to cry. "Why?" she asked.

"I was desperate," Yoni admitted. "And they offered me all this money, and I thought it was my chance to get out of here. But, listen, I don't want to get out of here anymore. I want to stay right here and finish our movie and make you a star. What do you say?"

Clara thought for a beat and then descended to the floor.

"Does this mean you're staying?" Yoni asked.

Clara nodded. "I'm staying."

Yoni grinned until he saw her eyes. The tears were gone, and in their place was fire.

• • •

Yoni coughed as he wandered through the rubble. The set hadn't fared well in the blaze. All that remained of the cobbler's shop were a few scraps of warped, ashy leather. The light fixtures had shattered, and the concrete floor was scorched beyond repair.

"Clara?" Yoni called out. "Come on, I know you're up there."

Clara lowered slowly from the ceiling. "Hey," she said.

"Hey," he said.

"I can't believe it was all bullshit," she said.

"I'm sorry," Yoni said.

"The script, the sets, the camera."

"I know."

She shook her head and sighed. She was still holding the fake copy of *Variety;* the pages were singed and crumbling.

"There's just one thing I don't get," she said. "How did you get the crew to react that time?"

"What do you mean?"

"When we rehearsed that new scene. And the crew was all nodding—"

"That wasn't fake," Yoni said.

Clara rolled her eyes.

"I swear," Yoni said. "They were on board."

"I don't buy it."

"Clara, you were there," Yoni said. "You remember. You felt it. We had them."

She smiled softly. "I guess we kind of did there for a moment."

Yoni surveyed the debris. "I really am sorry, Clara."

"It's all right," she said. "I guess I'm sorry too."

Yoni laughed. "For what?"

Clara pointed over Yoni's shoulder. He turned around and saw a tall golden man smiling down on him.

"Clara?" Yoni asked. "Did you murder me?"

"Oh yeah," Clara said. "Big-time."

"Be not afraid," the angel said to Yoni. "Your pain is finally coming to an end."

He held out his golden palm.

Clara rolled her eyes as Yoni slowly reached for it. He was about to make contact when he suddenly withdrew his hand.

"If it's cool with you," he told the angel, "I think I'd rather stay."

"What?" said the angel.

"I'd rather stay," Yoni repeated, his voice a little louder. He turned to Clara and saw that she was beaming.

"Whoa, whoa, whoa," said the angel. "Let's just talk about this."

"There's nothing to talk about," Yoni said. "I came to this town to make movies, and I'm not going to leave until I pull it off."

The angel turned angrily to Clara. "What did you do to him, Pamela?"

Yoni stepped between them. "Her name isn't Pamela," he said. "It's Clara Ginger."

The angel threw up his hands in frustration.

"How are you morons going to make a movie? You have no camera, no crew, and you live in a pile of ashes! You can't even move shit with your hands! You're a couple of fucking ghosts!"

"That's just a little hiccup," Clara said.

Yoni nodded. "Just another hurdle for us to jump over."

"You're both crazy," said the angel.

"Fuck you," Yoni said. "Eat my ass."

The angel cursed under his breath and flew back up to heaven.

"Nice work," Clara said. "I thought he'd never leave."

She slapped Yoni on the back and, to both of their surprise, made contact.

"Whoa," she said. "That's new."

She tentatively held out her palm. Yoni took her hand and gave it an exploratory squeeze. Their fingers clasped, and Yoni realized, with shock, that he was rising slowly with her off the ground.

"You're okay," she said, looking into his eyes. "Just don't look down."

Yoni and Clara floated upward toward the ceiling. Outside, the California sun was rising, flooding the gutted studio with light.

"Where do we start?" he asked.

"I don't know," Clara said. "Pitch me something."

Yoni let go of her hand and eagerly fanned out his palms. He looked like a bird taking flight.

"Okay," he said. *"Open on..."*

ACKNOWLEDGMENTS

I want to thank my wonderful agent, Daniel Greenberg, for believing in my writing all these years, even as it has gotten progressively weirder. Thanks also to my excellent editor, Michael Szczerban, and his hardworking colleagues at Little, Brown: Nicky Guerreiro, Alyssa Persons, Lauren Velasquez, and Karen Landry. Thanks to Susan Morrison and Emma Allen at *The New Yorker,* Jonathan Harvey at the BBC, and everyone at Serpent's Tail in London. Thank you, Lee Eastman, Gregory McKnight, Patricia O'Hearn, and Ed Steed,.

Lots of smart people have read and improved these stories over the years. In some instances, they read and gave notes on multiple versions of the same story. Sometimes, they spent hours talking to me on the phone about how to fix a story and are only finding out now, upon getting this book in the mail, that the story they worked so hard to improve is not even in the book, I just cut it in the end. Thank you, Jake Luce, Shana Gohd, and my very patient mother, Gail Winston.

Most of all, I want to thank my brilliant, talented wife, the author Kathleen Hale, who helped me in a lot of different ways, ranging from literally, physically writing some parts of the book to giving me a home and family. I love you.

South Dublin Libraries

www.southdublinlibraries.ie